THE
HIDDEN STONE
MYSTERY

Tom and Gulliver did not hear the faint creak of floor boards.

The Hidden Stone Mystery

A Tom Quest Adventure

THE HIDDEN STONE MYSTERY

By
FRAN STRIKER

WILDSIDE PRESS

Contents

CONTENTS

THE
HIDDEN STONE
MYSTERY

CHAPTER 1

The Headline

10:45 A.M.

The Pullman porter tucked his watch back into his vest pocket and reflected that the westbound train would leave the Cleveland station on schedule. He bent to pick up the square box that served as a bottom step, then looked in the direction of a shout:

"Hold that train!"

A tall, thin man carrying a small suitcase in one hand and a topcoat in the other was racing through the gate. It was Whiz Walton, whose daily newspaper column and feature articles were syndicated from coast to coast.

He bounded up the steps just as the train began to move, then paused in the vestibule to catch his breath as it gained headway.

"Close," he murmured, taking off his snap-brimmed hat and wiping his forehead with a carefully folded handkerchief from the breast pocket of his pin-striped suit.

The dusky porter grinned and said, "Sure was!" He slammed the door and fastened it.

"I hope," the columnist said as he tucked his handkerchief back into his pocket and adjusted it so three corners of it made symmetrical points, "that I'm on the right train."

The porter's eyes went wide. "You—you ain't sure?" he asked in surprise.

"There's room for doubt."

"If you'll let me see your ticket, suh—"

Whiz Walton shook his head and smiled wryly. "I didn't have time to get a ticket. I'll have to buy one from the conductor."

"You want to go to Chicago, suh?"

"Nope."

"Well, that's where this train is a-goin'."

"This is the right train if a certain passenger is on board. I'm looking for a young fellow named Tom Quest."

"Quest?" repeated the porter questioningly. "What's he look like?"

"A bit shorter than I am, but his shoulders are broader. He's dark-haired, about seventeen years old, looks a little older. A nice-looking fellow with a coat of tan you'd know he got in Mexico."

"Uh—Mexico?" The porter gulped.

"Well, part of it is from Mexico, but he had some left over from Ecuador and Florida."

The porter took off his cap and scratched the top of his head. "I jus' don' think I'd know the difference," he said somewhat apologetically. "My run's always been New York to Chicago. Now ef—"

The vestibule door swung open and Tom Quest called, "Whiz Walton!"

"Tom!" The columnist shot out his hand and met that of the boy in a firm grip.

"I saw you running for the train. I was in the second car forward. Golly, I was surprised. I thought you were in New York."

"I was. I caught a plane out at the crack of dawn this morning."

"This sure is a coincidence."

"This," the columnist said soberly, "is no coincidence. It's the result of a fast plane ride and a ten-buck bribe, so the cab driver would smash speed laws from the Cleveland airport to the station. They told me when I called your school that you had taken this train."

"You called the school?"

Whiz Walton grinned. "Got your headmaster out of bed at five A.M. He didn't like it, either."

The vestibule was noisy with the clattering of wheels,

the clanking of iron couplings, and the rattle of doors.

Whiz Walton picked up his suitcase and said, "Let's go inside. Have you had breakfast?"

"Two hours ago."

"I haven't. Come on into the diner while I grab a bite."

"I won't have much time," Tom replied. "I'm leaving the train at Lorraine. Dad has a little cottage near there. He's working on a book."

"I know all about it, Tom, and you have just as much time as I have. I'm leaving the train when you do."

"I'll take your bag, suh," said the porter, reaching. "I'll put it right in my car."

"Thanks," Whiz said. "You might as well take this, too." He tossed his topcoat over the porter's arm. "Now to get some breakfast."

Whiz Walton gave his order to the waiter in the dining car. "—And hurry it up," he added. "I'm leaving the train at Lorraine."

Then he lighted a cigarette, exhaled a stream of smoke toward the ceiling, and looked at Tom across the table.

"Curious?" he inquired.

Tom's face was extremely sober. "Whiz," he said, "there's something wrong, and I don't know what it is. What are you doing on this train? Why are you going to see my dad?"

"Did I say I was going to see Hamilton Quest?"

"No, but you're getting off the train at Lorraine, and I don't know of anyone else near there."

"Well, you're right, Tom. That's where I'm going."

"But why? What's wrong? Do you know why Dad sent for me?"

"How much do you know?"

"Yesterday afternoon," the boy replied as he picked up a spoon and traced a pattern on the snowy white tablecloth, "Doctor Parker called me into his office. He's my faculty counselor at school. He said that Dad had telephoned and asked if I could be dismissed from school for a few days. Doctor Parker said it would be all right for me to leave. The headmaster had already given his permission. I can make up my work when I get back."

"Did he tell you why your father sent for you?"

"No," Tom shook his head. "He said he had made a railroad reservation for me, and that one of the other teachers would drive me into New York so I could get this train."

The food arrived. Scrambled eggs and toast for Whiz together with a pot of coffee, and a glass of milk for Tom.

The reporter eyed the pattern Tom Quest had traced with the spoon handle on the tablecloth. It was a spiral with the outside end curled back at the bottom in a way that gave it a resemblance to a question mark. The same pattern, fashioned in gold, was mounted on a ring that Tom Quest wore on his finger.

That spiral had brought Tom and Whiz Walton together. Readers of *Sign of the Spiral* will remember how these two and Tom's friend Gulliver had followed the clue of the ring's pattern to capture a notorious gang whose hideout was beneath a western ghost town.

The spiral figured prominently in Tom Quest's life a second time during an adventure among the headhunters of Ecuador, as related in *The Telltale Scar*. Whiz Walton and Gulliver shared those jungle perils with Tom, as well as later adventures in the Florida Everglades and in the search for a lost city of ancient Aztecs in Mexico.

Full accounts of these expeditions are to be found in *The Clue of the Cypress Stump* and *The Secret of the Lost Mesa*.

Whiz Walton wolfed his food and washed it down with coffee.

"I guess," he mused, "I'm better informed than you are—and in a tougher spot."

"A tougher spot?" repeated Tom.

"A reporter or a columnist can't rest on his laurels."

"What do you mean, Whiz?"

"One mistake—one boner—can wipe out the work of years. Yesterday morning at this time I was on top of the world. Everything was fine. I filed a follow-up story on the Mandan Stone."

"The Mandan Stone!" Tom Quest cut in quickly. "That's the ancient stone that was discovered up in the Red River country. Dad was called up there to inspect it."

The reporter used his napkin, then nodded his head soberly.

"Does the Mandan Stone have anything to do with—with this trip?" Tom asked.

Whiz Walton nodded again. "Likewise," he said, "with my fall from the pinnacle."

"But how can that be?" Tom demanded. "It's been weeks since Dad inspected the stone."

"There is," said Whiz, "a lot that you don't know about that stone. Some of it came over the teletype at three o'clock this morning. That's when I decided I'd better get to your father in a hurry. And I wanted to see you before you saw the papers. I called your school and found out you'd already left."

"Where do you stand, Whiz? You said something about falling from a pinnacle."

"Never mind me. It's—" The reporter broke off abruptly, then in a low voice muttered, "Those lousy—"

Whiz was looking past Tom Quest, toward the end of the car. Tom started to turn in the direction of the newshawk's stare.

"Wait a minute, Tom." Whiz Walton placed a hand on the boy's arm. He was speaking rapidly. "I did my best to keep the story out of the papers. My own outfit promised to sit on it until I could check or at least get a statement from your father. Joe said he'd try to kill it in the other papers, but I guess he couldn't do it.

"It's a page-one headline, and it's a stinker. But get this, Tom. I don't believe it and we're going to make certain yellow journalists I know eat their words!"

Tom turned in his chair. A paper held open by a man at another table carried an eight-column banner on page one. Bold black type spelled out the name of Tom Quest's father, coupled with a shocking charge:

HAMILTON QUEST CALLED FRAUD.

CHAPTER 2

The Mandan Story

Tom quest couldn't believe it. Yet, there it was on the front page of a Cleveland paper. His father called a fraud!

Hot rage boiled up within the boy. Red spots danced before his eyes and the offensive headline seemed to dance and shimmer. His fists were clenched so tightly that the skin over the knuckles turned white.

Whiz Walton's voice came as from a great distance, saying, "Take it easy, Tom."

Tom turned toward the reporter. "Wha—what's it all about?" he faltered. "Dad is no fraud."

"There isn't a more sincere man in the world than your father, Tom. Everyone knows that."

Tom pushed back his chair and rose to his feet. "I'm going to borrow that paper," he said. "I want to read that story."

"Just a minute. Sit down. I'll tell you about it."

Tom resumed his seat. "I know that Dad is a little bit eccentric," he said. "I guess most scientists are like that. And I know that he doesn't make friends easily, but he's no fraud! Anyone who says he is—is a liar!"

"That article," said Whiz, "is in connection with the Mandan Stone."

"In that case I'm more than ever sure that the story is wrong. Dad is one of the world's top authorities on the Mandan Indians. Why, he's lived among them. He speaks their language. He was made a blood brother of Chief Wahkee. Why, he knows them as well as he knows—as he knows anyone."

The columnist nodded soberly. As Tom spoke, he recalled some of the strange things he had learned about the Mandan Indians from Hamilton Quest.

It was just about a year since Quest had returned after spending several months among the Mandans.

Including men, women, and children, there were about two thousand members in the tribe. They occupied a village on the west bank of the Missouri River about two hundred miles south of the mouth of the Yellowstone River, and held a legal claim to the property because of an old government land grant.

The Mandans had remained unmolested for hundreds of years, chiefly because they had nothing that anyone else could want. The expansion of civilization and industry that had overrun all the other Indian tribes had not come near the Mandans.

Poor soil and long, severe winters made the country undesirable for farming, and there were no natural resources in the form of timber, water power, or minerals to lure the grasping white men.

The Mandans were said to be the most ancient race of Indians in the United States, and claimed to be the first people created on earth.

While visiting them, Hamilton Quest had made some surprising discoveries. He found that many of the Indians had blond hair and blue eyes, and learned that they habitually made use of steam baths. In other things, too—their form of swimming, their use of food, and their language—there was a striking similarity to Scandinavians. Most striking of all was their language, which, unlike any other Indian tongue, had much in common with the language of the Welsh.

These discoveries had sent Quest to museums in many parts of the country, including the Smithsonian Institute in Washington. He delved deeply in old history books and ancient archives, especially those that dealt with Scandinavian countries. Finally, in an obscure paper, he learned that Magnus, King of Norway in the fourteenth century, had sent an expedition to explore the country west of Greenland.

Quest believed that members of this expedition had found their way to the region where the Mandans lived, and had gathered evidence to support his claim that these people from Norway had intermarried and that their descendants still lived in the Mandan village.

With many notebooks full of information, Tom's father had rented a small house in Ohio to prepare a book. He had taken with him the Quests' steadfast friend, Gulliver.

But there had been an interruption in the writing of the book. Hamilton Quest had been called back to the Mandan country to inspect a curious stone—the Mandan Stone.

"What about the Mandan Stone?" demanded Tom Quest. "What has that to do with a headline calling Dad a fraud?"

"Do you," asked Whiz Walton, "remember hearing of a man named Huddlebeck?"

"Of course I do," replied Tom. "Hector Huddlebeck is the head of the mining syndicate that found the Mandan Stone."

"That's right. His organization got a rather dubious title to some land adjoining the Mandan village, and started prospecting. The area previously had been looked over for gold, silver, copper, and other minerals. But Huddlebeck was prospecting for uranium."

"I know all about that," said Tom impatiently. "While they were digging they turned up a slab of stone with writing on it. That's when they sent for Dad. He went there and deciphered the writing.

"He told me all about it in a letter. The stone had been set up over a hundred years ago to mark the boundary of the land that had been given to the Indians by the government. Somehow it got buried, and the boundary line was indefinite. No one knew just where the boundary was, and no one cared until Huddlebeck went up there."

"That," said Whiz, "is where the trouble started. Your father, in deciphering the carving on the stone, proved that the syndicate had been digging on Mandan property. The uranium that they discovered belonged to the Indians."

"So what?" demanded Tom Quest.

"I guess you don't know what happened after that."

Tom shook his head.

"Well, Huddlebeck is not a man to take a setback. He had put a lot of money into the search for uranium, and wasn't going to lose it without a fight."

"If he's the one who called my dad a fraud—" began Tom hotly.

"Let me finish."

"Sorry, Whiz."

"Huddlebeck had the stone crated and shipped to a

New York State university where three of the world's foremost archeologists could examine it. Those men issued their reports last night. The story came over the teletype to my paper early this morning."

"What was their report?"

"That the letters had been chiseled into the stone quite recently with modern tools; and that the stone had been buried less than one year."

"But Dad said—" broke in Tom.

"Those three scientists agreed that your father was all wrong when he said the stone had been buried over a hundred years."

"Dad couldn't be that wrong!"

Whiz Walton shrugged his shoulders. "It's his word against that of three other men. And frankly, Tom, those three are just as well thought of in the scientific field as your father.

"You see, Huddlebeck has proved that the stone is a fake. Now he can go ahead and claim the uranium."

"By calling Dad a fraud!"

"He went farther than that, in the statement that came through last night—or rather this morning. Huddlebeck charges that your father knew about the uranium and helped the Indians plant the stone where it was sure to be found."

"Why in the world," demanded Tom explosively, "would Dad do anything like that!"

"Huddlebeck says that your father hopes to profit along with the Mandans. We're all behind the eight-ball, Tom. My feature story about the discovery of the stone was carried in the Sunday supplement of over three hundred newspapers all over the world.

"When word that the stone was a fake came through last night, my boss called me and raised blue blazes. Said that either I was a gullible jackass, or I was working in cahoots with your father to put over a flimflam on the Huddlebeck crowd."

"Oh, golly!" murmured Tom.

"Well, I," declared Whiz Walton aggressively, "am not gullible, and I'm not involved in any flimflam."

"Neither is my dad."

"Nevertheless, the word of those three men in the University is going to stand unless we do something about it."

"Do you suppose," asked Tom Quest quickly, "Huddlebeck has bribed them?"

The reporter shook his head. "I doubt it."

"Huddlebeck has a lot at stake."

"Those professors couldn't be bribed. If money interested them, they wouldn't be spending their time in the University. Furthermore, their reputations are at stake, too. Other scientists will inspect that stone."

"You—you think they'll agree with the professors, and say that Dad was wrong?"

"All I know is this. There's something mighty funny about the whole deal. That's why I'm going to call on your dad. I want the story first hand. I—" The reporter broke off sharply as something caught his eye.

Then he breathed, "Holy mackerel!"

Tom looked out the window. A jeep was running wide open less than fifty feet away on the highway that paralleled the railroad tracks. It was a jeep without a windshield. Rushing air flattened the wide brim of the driver's cowboy hat back against the crown. The driver was far too big for the car. He seemed to bulge over the sides, and the steering wheel was lost in his huge hands.

"It's Gulliver!" exclaimed Tom Quest.

The jeep was passing the train window and gaining on the locomotive. Two uniformed men on motorcycles were in hot pursuit.

"Oh, that crazy oaf!" groaned Whiz Walton. "As if we didn't have enough trouble! He's got to try to outrun motor cops!"

"I hope they don't start shooting at him," Tom said.

"If they do," observed the reporter, "Gulliver will probably pull out that oversized six gun of his and shoot back!"

The motorcycles were opposite the window where Whiz and Tom sat. Gulliver's jeep was well ahead. Whiz Walton couldn't see it from his side of the table, and

Tom had to lean close to the window and peer out at an acute angle.

"He'll be killed!" he exclaimed suddenly. "The highway makes a sharp turn up ahead and crosses the railroad tracks! Now he's on the turn! He's skidding!"

Whiz Walton rounded the table and pressed his cheek flat against the window over Tom's head. He caught a quick glimpse of Gulliver's jeep swaying wildly as it right-angled toward the train.

Tom and Whiz braced themselves, anticipating a crash. None came. As the train crossed the highway, it cut off the State Police, who braked their motor-cycles to a skidding stop.

The jeep was across the tracks, roaring on its way, and Gulliver was looking back and grinning.

A few moments later a conductor appeared at the end of the car and said, "Lorraine."

Whiz paid his fare and paid for his breakfast.

"This," he said, "is where we get off."

CHAPTER 3

Gulliver's Mission Accomplished

Hamilton quest was at the station in a small car to meet his son. He shook hands with Tom and welcomed the reporter warmly, too.

"I'm very glad to see you, Whiz," he said. "I suppose you have heard the news."

The columnist nodded soberly. "It came into the office early this morning," he said. "I took a plane to Cleveland and joined Tom on the train."

The scientist nodded. "A friend of mine at the University called me long distance yesterday." He turned toward his son. "I am confronted by an unpleasant situation, Tom."

"I know all about it, Dad. Whiz told me on the train."

"Oh."

The reporter said, "It's hit the stands, Mr. Quest. It's too big to suppress."

"In that case, there is little more to say until I get further information. Get into the car. We'll go to the cottage. Do you want to drive, Tom?"

The boy nodded and climbed into the driver's seat.

"Drive straight ahead. I'll tell you where to turn."

Tom shifted the gears and the car moved forward smoothly.

"It's about two miles to the cottage. You will like it. It's small, but very comfortable."

"Where do you stand, Dad?" Tom asked. "Could you possibly be mistaken about the Mandan Stone?"

Hamilton Quest shook his head slowly, saying, "I was not mistaken."

"Then those men at the University—"

"I know all three of them," replied the older man, "and I am convinced that their decision is quite right."

"Someone must be wrong!" put in Whiz Walton.

"Not necessarily."

"But Dad," said Tom, "how do you figure—"

"There can be but one answer, Tom. The stone that was sent to the University is not the stone that I examined."

"That's it!" said Whiz. "That's the answer! That's a

statement for the press! Have you talked to any other newsmen?"

"No. I have given out no statements."

"Then let me release one."

"Not yet, Whiz. Wait until I am sure that my theory is correct. Turn here to the right, Tom," he added.

Tom swung the car into a dirt road bordered by shady maple trees.

"Are you," asked Whiz, "doing anything to prove your theory?"

"When I examined the stone in the Mandan village, I marked it, as I do all such specimens, so that I might identify it later."

"How did you mark it?"

"Using a pointed tool, I scratched a mark in one corner on the reverse side of the stone. I made a little spiral." Quest smiled. "My favorite symbol—the sign of Archimedes.

"When my friend at the University telephoned to tell me what his associates had decided, I made up my mind to send Gulliver to inspect the stone they have, and photograph it."

"Gulliver!" repeated Tom.

"You sent him!" asked the reporter.

"Yes. Why?"

"We saw him from the train."

"You did? It doesn't seem possible that he can have returned so soon."

"He was heading this way," Tom insisted, "one jump ahead of a couple of motorcycle cops. They were State Police."

"Then he probably will be at the cottage waiting for us. He will have gone by the main highway. It is shorter than this route."

"If he's there," observed Whiz Walton dryly, "he's probably in handcuffs and leg irons. And if he's not there, we'll probably find him in the nearest jail."

"How could there be two stone slabs?" asked Tom.

"Very simple. The one that was shipped from the Mandan village is a crude imitation of the original. I might add it probably was especially crude, and intentionally so."

"I get it!" said Whiz Walton. "That big shot, Hector Huddlebeck, must have had the fake stone made up in a hurry and sent in place of the real one, just to discredit you!"

"We," said Hamilton Quest, "had better withhold our conclusions until we learn what Gulliver has to report." He paused, then turned toward his son. "The cottage, Tom, is just beyond the next turn to the left."

The dirt road joined the main highway at a right angle. The area was thickly wooded and sparsely settled. Hamilton Quest had rented a small one-story cottage painted green and white, set in a half-acre clearing. It faced the broad four-lane highway, and from the front porch offered a splendid view of Lake Erie. Tom Quest, approaching from the rear, swung off the dirt road and braked to a stop.

Hamilton Quest stepped out of the car. The others followed after they had lifted their bags from the rear seat.

"I thought Gulliver would be here ahead of us," Tom said.

"He certainly was *traveling*," Whiz agreed. "But the law probably caught up with him and told him to keep right on going until he reached the courthouse."

Hamilton Quest had taken a key case from his pocket. Selecting one, he said, "We will have to go around to the front door. The rear door is bolted from the inside with one of those chain contrivances."

"Lead the way," said Whiz.

The grass was green and well cared for, and flowering shrubs made an attractive cover for the foundation of the house. Tom was glad to note that his father had comfortable quarters.

"Oh, there he is!" Hamilton Quest said suddenly.

Rounding the side of the house, Tom saw that Gulliver's jeep had been driven off the highway and halted on the shoulder in front of the house. One motorcycle was parked ahead of the small car, and another one behind. Two uniformed men were talking to Gulliver.

"Yo', Tom!" boomed the big man heartily when he caught sight of his young friend. "An' Whiz Walton! Great day, come over here an' lemme see yo'!"

The invitation was hardly necessary. Tom and Whiz dropped their bags on the grass and hurried past Tom's father to greet Gulliver.

Gulliver was always an awe-inspiring sight. He was a huge man who stood six and a half feet tall without his boots on. His chest was broad and so deep that his torso seemed to have proportions like a barrel. His head seemed to rise from his shoulders with no neck in between, and his eyes were small and deep-set beneath thick eyebrows that came together above his broken nose to make a solid hedge at the base of a sloping forehead.

Gulliver owned a small ranch in Texas, where he had been born and brought up. He often boasted of his wrestling bouts with steers and wild horses. His face bore many scars of battle, some sustained in rodeo contests, others in fights with savages and natives in many remote parts of the Western Hemisphere. In age, the giant was halfway between Tom Quest and his father.

He had been a trusted companion on many of Hamilton Quest's explorations, and had at times assumed full responsibility for Tom's well-being. There had been one long period of ten years, soon after Tom's mother died, when Gulliver had acted as both father and mother to the boy.

"Gosh, Gulliver, it sure is good to see you!" exclaimed Tom. "In spite of—"

"You old troglodyte!" put in Whiz Walton. "What sort of a caper is this? Why are you sitting there? Get out of the jeep!"

"I can't," said Gulliver.

The rear seat of the jeep had been removed, and Gulliver was seated on the floor in the small space behind the front seats. His broad beam filled it completely and his legs were straight out.

"He refuses to budge," put in one of the red-faced members of the State Police.

The other turned to Hamilton Quest and said, "Mr. Quest—"

"What seems to be the difficulty, officer?"

It was Gulliver who answered. "I'm travelin' along, mindin' my own business on the way back from that there errand yo' wanted done. I hear a siren, an' lookin' back, I see these two young fellows comin' after me."

"You were doing seventy-five miles an hour!" cut in the smaller of the troopers.

"Aw-w-w, now, son," said Gulliver with a facial distortion that was supposed to be a disarming grin, "yo' ought t'know blamed well that these here jeeps can't go that fast."

"Our speedometers are checked every few days. We know how fast you were going. You've got that crate souped up!"

"Well, maybe just a mite or so."

"And you have no muffler!" cut in the other officer.

"What's more," said the first, "your driving was reckless. You almost rammed head-on into a train!"

"Aw-w shucks," the big man said, "I got across them tracks in plenty o' time, an' anyhow, if I had smacked into her, it wouldn't o' been head-on. The road was sideways to the tracks."

"Are you going to get out of that car or not?"

Gulliver placed his hands on the sides of the jeep as another person might rest his elbows on the gunwales of a canoe. He shifted his weight slightly and the movement brought protesting sounds from the jeep's springs.

"Uh-uh," he said. Then to Hamilton Quest, "I don't know what more these critters want. I showed 'em half a dozen drivers' licenses in different states, an' a permit to pack my shootin' iron."

"I'll assume the responsibility for what he has done." Hamilton Quest said to the officers.

The uniformed men seemed to know and respect

Hamilton Quest. One of them said, "He should at least get a ticket for speeding."

"Give it to me and I shall see that the fine is paid."

"Aw, skip it, Joe," the taller trooper said as the other man took out a pencil. "We'll let the big gorilla off this time, on account of Mr. Quest, but—" he turned to Gulliver "—the next time we see you breaking the speed laws, we'll run you in!"

Gulliver nodded agreeably and said, "Sure thing, boys. That'll be all right."

The man called Joe said, "Now that it's all settled, will you do a favor for me?"

"That depends on what yo' want."

"Get up so I can look at you. I'd like to see if you're as big as I think you are."

"What's it to yo'?"

"My cousin's a match-maker in Cleveland. I'll bet he'd like to know you."

"A match-maker!" exploded Gulliver, one eye squinted at the trooper. "Son," he continued, "I've steered clear o' match-makin' all my life, an' I don't hanker to git matched up now. I c'n handle my weight in men, wild bulls, or wildcats, but a hundred pounds o' she-male with match-makin' notions is one too many."

"I'm not talking about that kind of matching. I'm talking about wrestling. You could be built up as the Missing Link."

Hamilton Quest stepped forward, smiling. "I'm afraid he has no time for wrestling. He is going on a trip for me."

The trooper nodded, muttering, "I'd still like to see him standing up."

The two officers moved to their motorbikes, kicked up the supports, and stepped on the starters. As they roared off down the highway, Tom asked, "What's the matter, Gulliver? Can't you get out of the jeep?"

Whiz Walton said, "What are you doing in the back, anyway? How did you get there?"

"I was beginnin'," said Gulliver, "to have a fancy time with them two. I got here a couple o' jumps ahead o' them an' I'd just time enough to climb over from the driver's seat. That match-makin' critter was cussed stubborn about wantin' me to git out. At one time," Gulliver chuckled at the recollection, "he grabbed my arm an' tried to pull."

"That," observed Whiz Walton dryly, "was probably a mistake."

"Why are you sitting there?" demanded Tom.

"I'm hidin' it."

"You're hiding what?"

"What I'm sittin' on. I figured there might o' been a radio flash, or somethin' o' the sort, that'd make those fly-cop boys ask no end o' questions if they seen what I had in the jeep."

"What have you?" Hamilton Quest asked.

Gulliver's eyebrows lifted in surprise. "Gosh," he said, "yo' oughta know. Yo' sent me for it."

Hamilton Quest grew pale. "I—I sent you for what?" he asked in a thin voice.

"That hunk o' stone." Gulliver drew up his feet and scrambled over the side of the jeep.

Where he had been sitting there lay a slab of smooth stone slightly smaller than a curbstone. It was about two inches in thickness, nearly thirty inches long, and half as wide.

Gulliver gestured toward it and said with a touch of pride, "Yo' told me yo'd like to examine that stone real close."

Tom and Whiz saw the older man pass one thin hand across his forehead and his eyes. "Gulliver," Hamilton Quest said patiently, "I gave you a camera. I put a film into the camera, and I showed you how to use it. I asked you to go to the University, to speak to Professor Judson, and ask permission to photograph the stone."

"That critter!" Gulliver began. "He had no end o' questions. He wanted to know who I was, an' where I come from."

Whiz Walton spoke in a low voice, saying, "It's not hard to understand why a scientist would have an anthropological interest in you."

"Didn't you," asked Hamilton Quest, "say that I sent you?"

"It wasn't none o' his business. He got kind o' frothy with me. Then them two other critters joined us, an' when they heard I wanted to take pictures o' the stone, they got as touchy as a couple o' teased snakes. One o' them took my camera an' took out the film. That riled me."

There was an audible groan from Tom's father. "Then what?" he asked falteringly.

"I couldn't git no pictures, so I had to do the next best thing. I brought the stone itself."

"Didn't Judson and the other men try to stop you?"

Gulliver nodded and said, grinning, "They tried."

"I wonder," interjected Whiz, "if they'll recover."

"I didn't hurt 'em none. I just tucked 'em into a little closet in the corner an' swung the door closed on 'em."

"Locked them in, eh?"

"There wasn't no lock on the door, but there was an iron safe standin' in the room where they had that stone. I wheeled the safe across the door, then I tucked the stone under my arm, an' brought it here."

"Tucked it under his arm!" The columnist said to Tom, "If it weighs an ounce, it weighs a hundred and fifty pounds!"

Gulliver was lifting the stone from the jeep. "Now

where do yo' want it?" he inquired of Tom's father.

Hamilton Quest said, "Inasmuch as it *is* here, you had better bring it into the house. I shall telephone the University and try to square things."

"Look!" Tom Quest cried suddenly, pointing to the house.

The others turned quickly. The front door was wide open. In it stood a big man in brown dungarees and matching shirt. He was hatless and his blond hair was stained with blood which ran down the right side of his face. He staggered forward across the small porch, reaching with arms outstretched like a blind man.

"Stop!" called Tom. "Look out for those steps!"

The man appeared to neither see nor hear. At the top step, one foot reached into space and then the man pitched headlong to the flagstone walk.

"Who is he?" demanded Whiz Walton, running toward the fallen man.

"I don't know!" replied Hamilton Quest. "The house was locked when I left here an hour ago!"

CHAPTER 4

The Mysterious
Stranger

GULLIVER dropped the heavy slab on the soft grass and shouldered past Hamilton Quest and Tom.

"Lemme look at him," he said, squatting beside the unconscious man who lay face down on the flagstone walk.

With hands that were surprisingly gentle, he turned the man face up and felt deftly for a pulse.

"Is he alive?" asked Whiz Walton.

Gulliver grunted affirmatively.

"Who is he?"

Hamilton Quest responded. "I don't know. I never saw him before."

"How did he get into your house?"

31

"I don't know that either, Whiz. I am sure the door was locked when I left."

Gulliver had transferred his attentions to an ugly gash on the stranger's head. "Yo', Tom," he said, "scoot inside to my bedroom. It's the one in the back. Yo'll find my old medicine chest at the foot o' my bunk."

"No, no!" exclaimed Whiz Walton. "Not that." His past experiences with Gulliver's remedies had made him wary and distrustful. "Don't use any of the stuff in your chest. You'll kill the poor devil."

Gulliver ignored the suggestion. "Go on, Tom," he said. "Fetch out number fifty-two, which is a sort of antiseptic, an' number sixteen to bring the critter conscious. An' while yo're at it, yo' better fetch along some tape an' bandage. Likewise scissors."

"Are there scissors in your chest?" asked Tom.

"Yo'll find somethin' I c'n use to cut away the hair close to the wound. I don't know about small scissors, but they's a pair o' tin snippers—"

"Tin snippers," groaned Whiz Walton.

"Maybe a razor'd be better," muttered Gulliver, studying the injury.

Tom said, "I'll find something."

He mounted the steps three at a time, crossed the porch, and entered the house.

As soon as Tom Quest entered the large living room,

he had a feeling that something was not as it should be. He paused and looked around. Everything appeared to be in order. Chairs, tables, lamps, and other articles were in place. The carpet was unscuffled. There was nothing to indicate that a struggle had taken place.

The boy hurried through a short hall to a small bedroom in the rear. It was crowded, but neat. At one side a small bed stood close to the wall. At the foot of the bed there was a battered wooden chest about two feet in all dimensions. It was heavily reinforced and bound with straps of iron.

Gulliver's chest was a relic of the distant past. It held all of the big man's important possessions. Wherever Gulliver went, the chest went with him. It had been designed originally as a medicine chest to be carried on a sailing vessel, and had been stocked with unguents, pills, and liquids of dubious character for the treatment of practically any ailment.

Most of the old-time skippers, who had to act in the capacity of doctor for their crews, used a chest of remedies like Gulliver's. To simplify the use of the medicines, each item was labelled with a number instead of a name, and the book of instructions that accompanied each chest described the symptoms of practically every ailment.

When a seaman was taken ill, the ship's captain

scanned his book until he found the symptoms that suited the case, then followed the instructions as to dosage. These instructions had been vague at best. "A pinch of number five placed on the end of the tongue"; or "As much of number thirty-two as can be heaped on a half-eagle"; or, in the case of liquids, the dose might be "two fair swallows."

Gulliver somehow had come into possession of the chest in the course of his many travels. Some of the containers still held medicines. Gulliver had never seen the book of instructions, but by trial and error through the years, he had found a use for practically everything the chest held.

A salve, for example, pale yellow in color, had proved to be excellent for polishing boots and belts and other leather articles. A mysterious bright-red liquid worked well as gun oil, and there were various uses for the other items.

Much had been added to the chest's original contents. There were jars, small cans, and bottles filled with hot peppers, spices, and other condiments that Gulliver particularly favored in his cooking to give his food "authority." There were spare parts for the jeep—spare guns and ammunition; oil, grease, and cleaning rags; a box of assorted nails, screws, nuts, and bolts; a hammer, a screwdriver, and other tools. The chest also held concentrated food in tablet form and a small blue book with a paper cover called, touchingly enough, *Recipes Every Bride Should Know.*

Tom found the bottles labelled "52" and "16," and placed them on the floor. He pushed aside an empty holster attached to a gun belt and an unattached holster that held a Colt revolver. He dug beneath a number of other personal possessions and finally found a roll of bandage wrapped in blue paper, and a spool of white adhesive tape. He could find no scissors, but in a toilet kit he located a straight razor which would serve for cutting the wounded man's hair.

By the time he had rejoined his friends outside, the stranger was stirring uneasily.

"We may not need number sixteen," Gulliver informed Tom Quest. "He's comin' around without it."

"How about his wound?" asked Tom.

"It ain't so deep, an' the bleedin's stopped. I'll just cut the hair away an' douse it with some fifty-two. I reckon he'll be all right."

Tom looked at his father, who nodded approval of Gulliver's first aid.

"He seems to have been struck on the head with a club of some sort," Hamilton Quest said.

"A blunt instrument," put in Whiz Walton.

"Has he said anything?" Tom asked.

"Not yet. He's trying to get his bearings."

Using the razor, Gulliver proceeded to cut off the blond hair close to the wound. "Soon as I'm done," he said, "I'll carry him inside where we c'n wash him up an' put him to bed."

Tom tried to remember what it was that had impressed him when he first entered the cottage. It was something that had sounded a warning note—something had registered in his mind, but his mind, at the time, had been full of other things. There remained only that vague and elusive sensation of something forgotten.

Which one of his senses had caught the warning? Was it something he had seen or heard? He couldn't remember having heard any sounds other than his own footsteps during his brief stay in the house, nor could he remember seeing anything out of order, or anything that seemed incongruous.

He had caught the warning in the living room. He remembered the living room with his father's desk in one corner and comfortable, well-worn chairs with tables conveniently at hand, and lamps. Perhaps if he went back to the room—

"While Gulliver is working on the man," he said, "I'll carry in the suitcases."

When no one replied, Tom crossed the lawn to where he and Whiz Walton had dropped their bags. He picked them up and went through the front door a second time.

As soon as he crossed the threshold he knew what it was that had struck a note of strangeness. It was nothing he had seen or heard. It was something he had smelled—an acrid odor that had no place in the well-ordered, peaceful home of a dignified scientist at work on a book. It was an odor commonly associated with violence and crime, with war and bloodshed, and with sudden death. It was the odor of burned gunpowder. Someone, quite recently, had fired a gun inside the house.

Tom placed the suitcases in a corner of the living room and looked for further signs of gunfire. He could see no bullet holes in either walls or woodwork. The ceiling was an unblemished expanse of white. The floor was covered with gray carpeting from wall to wall.

Tom eyed it hurriedly at first, then carried his search farther by looking behind and beneath each piece of furniture. He moved three chairs and found nothing. Then he moved the fourth chair—a large one with wide, well-padded arms and seat. On the floor where the chair had concealed it, lay a gun.

Tom picked the weapon up with his handkerchief so that he would not spoil any fingerprints that might be on it. He recognized the weapon instantly. It had a fancy handle, one that Gulliver had made himself from the horns of an antelope.

Tom remembered the empty holster in his big friend's medicine chest. That was where the gun had nestled, until someone within the past hour had taken it from the chest and fired it inside the house.

"What have you there?"

Tom turned quickly toward the door as his father entered. "It's a gun," replied the boy. "One of Gulliver's, and it's been fired in this room. Smell the powder?"

Hamilton Quest looked deeply concerned.

"Be careful of fingerprints!" said Whiz Walton, coming through the door.

"I'm being careful, Whiz. I haven't touched the gun. I've kept my handkerchief around it."

Gulliver's voice boomed from outside. "Lemme through or I'll put this critter on the porch."

Hamilton Quest and the columnist moved to one side. Gulliver came in with the wounded man in his arms.

"He's passed out again," he said to Tom as he crossed the living room. "I'll put him on my bed an' give him a couple o' whiffs o' number sixteen. That should do the trick."

Carrying the revolver, Tom accompanied Gulliver to the rear of the house, followed by his father and Whiz Walton. The discovery of the weapon had added many questions to those that had arisen when the mysterious stranger stumbled from the house.

CHAPTER 5

Gulliver's Gun

THE BLOND MAN in dungarees regained consciousness while Hamilton Quest was washing away the blood that had dried on his face and hair.

"Just take it easy," the explorer said gently. "You're going to be all right."

"You are—Mr. Quest?" the stranger asked in a faltering voice.

"That's right. You were struck on the head, but it's not serious, and you are going to be all right. Don't try to talk until you have regained some of your strength."

The other nodded. "I—got plenty to—to tell you." He paused for a long moment. "H-h-head," he said painfully, "head is spinning."

"Just rest for a little while. I'll stay here with you."

In the meantime, Tom Quest and Gulliver stood close to Whiz Walton, who sat at the desk in the living room examining Gulliver's thirty-eight. He held it gingerly on a pencil inserted in the barrel, squinting at it from various angles.

"Offhand," he stated, "I'd say that whoever used this gun wiped it clean so there would be no fingerprints."

He placed the gun on the desk pad and snubbed his cigarette in an ashtray, adding, "I'll make sure."

Using the round, smooth end of the cap of his fountain pen, he pulverized the ashes from several cigarettes until they were reduced to a very fine gray powder. This he dumped from the ashtray to a sheet of paper, then carefully dusted the pistol.

"Finely powdered cigarette ash," he explained, "makes a first-rate fingerprint powder. If there are any fingerprints on this gun, the powder will show them up."

"All this shilly-shallyin' about fingerprints," observed Gulliver. "I don't see any point in it. No one was shot by that gun, so what difference does it make if they's fingerprints on 'er?"

"How do you know no one was shot?" demanded the reporter.

"Whiz," said Gulliver, "in the first place, when a man is shot, they's generally red stains around, an' also a corpse. In the second place, that there gun wouldn't kill no one unless the sidewinder who borrowed it without permission dumped out the shells that were in it an' replaced 'em with others."

"What do you mean by that?" asked the columnist.

"Lemme take the gun. I'll show yo'."

Whiz Walton had finished his experiment with cigarette ash, and confirmed his opinion that the gun had been wiped clean.

"Go ahead," he said. "Take it."

Gulliver picked up the revolver by the handle and with a deft flip dropped the cylinder sideways. He touched the ejector and six shells dropped to the desk. One of these was empty. Five held powder, but there was a wad of paper where lead bullets should have been.

"Yo' see," said Gulliver, "these here is blank cartridges."

"Blanks!" exclaimed Tom Quest. "How come? What were you doing with blanks in your gun?"

"I put 'em in about a month or so ago to throw a scare into a two-legged hyena that'd been prowlin' around the woods near this here house, but I never got a chance to use 'em because he never came back."

Tom Quest said, "Do you suppose the one who used this gun knew it was loaded with blanks?"

Gulliver shook his head. "I doubt it."

"So do I," put in Whiz Walton. "I think he used the

gun intending to kill someone—probably the fellow who got cracked on the head."

"Even blanks," said Tom, "would make a mark. The powder specks would show if the gun was fired reasonably close to anyone."

"Doggone," said Gulliver. "Maybe they do show! I was so busy lookin' at the wound on that man's head, I never thought o' lookin' for anythin' else. I'll look now."

Gulliver hurried to the back bedroom with Tom and Whiz. The stranger was awake, and color had returned to his face.

"He feels much better," Hamilton Quest said. "He has a lot to say, but he's been saving it until we could all hear the story at the same time."

"Lemme look at him," said Gulliver, pulling back a blanket. "Lemme look at his back."

Gulliver addressed the stranger. "Turn over face down for a minute. We got to look for somethin'."

The stranger obeyed without comment.

"There," said Gulliver, pointing to an area between the shoulder blades. On the brown shirt hundreds of tiny spots formed a circle about eight inches in diameter.

"Yo'd never notice that," said Gulliver, "unless yo' were lookin' for it."

"That looks like a powder burn," observed Tom's father.

"That's what it is, an' if my gun had held a bullet instead o' blanks, this here gent would be an interestin' subject for the undertaker, an' we'd be answerin' questions to the cops."

The stranger turned on his back again. "You—you mean to say that someone shot at me?"

"Yo're doggoned right, an' with my gun!"

The stranger's face went white, then red. "That dirty —" he began in a low voice. "I didn't think he'd go that far."

"Who?" demanded Whiz Walton.

"My partner." The man's hand reached into a pocket of the dungarees and brought out a business card. "Here," he said, handing it to Hamilton Quest, "this is our firm."

It was a cheap card. "*Gates and Gleason, Trucking*," it read.

"I'm Gates," the injured man explained. "Gleason is my partner—or was until we broke up. He—he's the one who slugged me. I didn't think he'd try to kill me."

"But what were you doing in this house?" Whiz Walton asked. "And why did Gleason slug you?"

Gates said, "It's a long story. I'll make it as short as I can. It started when we were hired to haul a hunk of stone from an Indian village to the University."

"The Mandan Stone!" exclaimed Tom Quest. "Golly,

I'd forgotten all about it! It's still out on the front lawn where Gulliver dropped it!"

"Me," said Gulliver, "I forgot 'er, too."

"Bring it into the house," said Hamilton Quest. "Meanwhile, I'd better put in a call to the University and try to square things with Professor Judson and his colleagues. Then we'll hear what else Gates has to say."

CHAPTER 6

The Truck Driver's Story

GULLIVER handled the hundred-and-fifty-pound slab of stone as easily as a man of average strength might handle a schoolboy's slate. He brought it into the house and stood it on end against a wall in the living room, where Hamilton Quest could examine it at leisure.

Meanwhile, the archeologist had put through a call to Professor Judson and learned that the three men whom Gulliver had imprisoned in a closet had been released after a few minutes of shouting and hammering on the door.

Professor Judson at first had been almost incoherent with anger, but became mollified when Hamilton Quest explained that Gulliver's bold action sprang from unswerving loyalty.

"Well, Quest," Professor Judson finally said, "I suppose my colleagues and I must make allowances. After all, no harm has been done."

"No harm," remarked Hamilton Quest drily, "except to my reputation."

"We're all sorry about that," said Professor Judson. "We, of course, knew what you had said about the Mandan Stone, and for the sake of your reputation we would have given you the benefit of any doubt, but as soon as we examined the specimen, we knew that there could be no doubt about the fact that you were entirely mistaken when you said it had been buried for a hundred years, and that the lettering had been cut into the face of the stone a century ago."

"One moment," broke in Hamilton Quest. "The stone you examined is in my home. I have not had a chance to study it carefully, but a casual glance is all I need to know that this is a different stone from the one I saw in the Mandan village."

There was no reply from Professor Judson.

"Well? Don't you believe me?" demanded Hamilton Quest.

The only response was a soft chuckle.

Quest's face was red with anger. "Why, confound you, Judson," he said, "I'd like to ram your suspicions down your throat!"

"Frankly," Professor Judson said, "it is hard to believe that a stone such as you described ever existed. The whole thing sounds like a scheme to defraud the Huddlebeck syndicate out of its property."

"The stone did exist, and I saw it. I examined it carefully. I handled it. I scratched a mark of identification on it."

"Then you could do your reputation a lot of good, Quest, by finding it again," Judson said soberly.

"And so I shall!" Tom's father said hotly. He slammed the phone into its cradle.

Tom had entered the room unnoticed by his father, and had heard most of the conversation. He had never seen the older man so shaken by rage and indignation.

"Golly, Dad—" he began.

Hamilton Quest turned quickly. "That—that—fool! He actually thinks I'd be stupid enough to try to put over a humbug and a flimflam! Why, he—he—" The explorer, unused to violent outbursts, was at a loss for words to express his feelings.

Gulliver came to his aid. "He's a triple-twisted, double-distilled jackass!" the big man began. "I took a dislike to the mealy-mouthed coyote as soon as I set eyes on him. He an' them other pasty-faced pismires put me in mind o' somethin' yo' find crawlin' around on putrefyin' ground beneath a heavy rock! Yo' told him yo'd find the real Mandan Stone. Well, by thunderation, me an' Tom an' Whiz will help yo' find it! An' when we do, I'll take it back to that there University an' rub the noses o' them critters ag'in the roughest part until the fronts o' their faces are polished as smooth as the bottom side of a new flatiron!"

Despite his anger, Hamilton Quest smiled at the big man's explosion. "Gulliver," he said, "there is no need—"

"Don't shush me! I'm just gittin' goin'!"

"Save the rest." It was Whiz Walton who spoke from the doorway. The columnist, until now, had been with Gates, the injured truckman.

"Let's get the rest of Gates' story," he suggested. "I, for one, would like to hear it."

They found Gates sitting in a chair in Gulliver's bedroom. He said that aside from a slight headache he felt fine.

Hamilton Quest sat in the only other chair, while Gulliver perched on his medicine chest. Tom sat on the bed near the foot, and Whiz Walton lay back on the pillows and lighted a cigarette.

Gates said, "Gleason and I trucked for Interstate Freight until about a year ago when we quit and pooled our cash to buy a truck of our own. We had big plans, and figured on buyin' more trucks and expandin'. We didn't do very well. There were a lot of expenses we hadn't counted on. Insurance and licenses were more than we had expected.

"We didn't have any reserve cash and pretty soon we got behind in our truck payments and insurance and everything else. It seemed like the only thing to do was to sell out for whatever cash we could get for the equity in the truck.

"We stuck an ad in a couple of newspapers. The first day the ad appeared, we had a phone call from a guy who said he might be interested. Gleason went to call on him while I hung around the office in case business came in.

"When Gleason came back, he had good news. The man he talked to had a special truckin' assignment. It called for one trip from the Mandan Indian country to a university in New York state. It was the longest haul we'd ever had, and it would pay us mighty well. In fact, we were to be paid about five or six times the usual mileage rate for such a haul. That one job would mean that we could pay off the balance we owed on the truck and stay in business.

"I suspected there was somethin' phony about the deal when Gleason told me how much the customer was payin'. I thought we were goin' to be asked to carry somethin' illegal, but Gleason said the whole deal was strictly on the level. He showed me some newspaper articles our client had handed to him. They told about you, Mr. Quest—"

"About me?"

Gates nodded. "One of them told how you had visited the Mandan Indians to inspect a slab of stone and how the Huddlebeck syndicate stood to lose a uranium discovery because of what you found on that stone."

Tom's father nodded. "I remember the article," he said.

"There was another article sayin' that this stone was to be sent to a university so's some other men could see if you were right."

Hamilton Quest colored slightly at this statement.

"All we had to do was pick up the stone, which was to be in a wooden crate, and take it to this university. I couldn't see where there was anything crooked about a deal like that."

Hamilton Quest shook his head slowly and said, "There wasn't."

"What," demanded Whiz Walton, "has all this to do with coming to this house and getting your head cracked open?"

"I'll get to that in a minute," replied Gates. "Gleason and I picked up the stone in our truck and started out. We decided to take turns sleeping and keep the truck going night and day until we reached our destination. I started out at the wheel. I'd gone about two hundred miles. I was on a deserted stretch of highway and travelin' at night. There was a big car about a quarter of a mile ahead of me. Suddenly the driver turned and blocked the road. I had to jam on the brakes to keep from smashin' into him. Then a couple of men stepped from each side of the road and pulled open the doors of the cab and held guns on me. They shook Gleason awake and held a gun on him, too. They told us to keep still and we wouldn't get hurt. I was plenty scared, so I kept still.

"There were other men in the gang. They went around to the back of the truck. I couldn't see what they were doing, of course, but I could hear them moving around inside and talking in low voices.

"After about five minutes, which seems like an hour when you're lookin' into the business end of a gun, one of the men came around and spoke to a guy who seemed to be the leader. I heard him say somethin' about 'the wrong truck.' They told me I could go on about my business, but I'd better keep my trap shut.

"By this time the car that had cut me off had pulled out of the way, so I put the truck in gear and shoved on.

"Well, that's about all there was to it at the time. We delivered the wooden crate to the University and got our pay for the job."

"Please get to the point," Whiz Walton said impatiently, as he snubbed out his cigarette in an ashtray. "You still haven't told us anything."

"The point," said Gates, "is simply this. Those men who stopped us did *not* get the wrong truck. They got the truck they wanted. While some of the gang held guns on us, others lifted off the stone we had picked up in the Mandan village and substituted another."

"The ornery sidewinders!" exclaimed Gulliver.

"So that's it," Tom Quest said.

Whiz Walton swung his long legs, which had been stretched out on the bed, to the floor. He said, "Who hired you, Gates? Who hired you to move that stone?"

"I don't know," said Gates. "Gleason made the deal and got the dough in cash. I don't even know the address of the man where Gleason went to talk to him."

"It's Huddlebeck," guessed Tom Quest. "He must have been behind it. He arranged to substitute a fake stone to discredit Dad. The worst of it is, he's gotten away with it. Now his syndicate can keep the title to that property where they found the uranium."

"How did you learn all this?" asked Whiz Walton.

Gates said, "Gleason was in on the whole deal. He knew from the start what they were planning to do. He told me about it today. You see, the two of us were driving through Cleveland. We stopped for lunch and bought a paper. Your name—" he nodded at Hamilton

Quest, "—was in the headlines. Gleason started bragging to me how he had helped to make those headlines. When I heard about the crooked deal, I told him I was coming here to see you."

"How," asked Hamilton Quest, "did you know where I lived?"

"It was in the paper. Gleason tried to talk me out of it. When he couldn't, he said he'd come with me. He said he was sorry about it, and would make a clean breast of the whole thing. I believed him then, but I can see now that he had entirely different plans.

"We started out—me driving. I remember leaving Cleveland and getting about halfway to Lorraine, and that's all I do remember. Gleason said to stop the truck for a second. I pulled over on the shoulder of the road and stopped, then something hit me on the head. Next thing I knew, I was on the floor in your living room. I got up, opened the door, and saw all of you outside."

"That's where we came in," observed Whiz Walton.

"I cannot imagine why Gleason brought you here," said Hamilton Quest.

"Or," put in Tom, "why he'd want to shoot you. That's going pretty far."

"It's goin' too far," rumbled Gulliver, "especially when he uses my gun!"

"Offhand," Whiz Walton said, "it looks as if he tried

to frame a murder either on Hamilton Quest or on Gulliver."

"If we can find Gleason, we may learn a few things."

"Maybe," said Tom hopefully, "we could get a confession out of him. That might clear Dad."

"The story Gates just told would go a long way toward clearing your father, Tom," Whiz Walton said. He turned to the truck driver. "Would you be willing to repeat that story under oath and sign it?"

Gates nodded. "I'll do anything I can to help you," he said. "Furthermore, I've got a score to settle with Gleason."

Tom's father shook his head slowly. "For the present," he said, "I want to keep this quiet. If I release a statement claiming that the original stone was stolen, people will say that I am simply making a feeble attempt to refute the charge of fraud."

"But Dad," said Tom Quest, "the Mandan Stone has been stolen! And this man's story will prove it."

"It would take more than his unsubstantiated story, son. I think I have a better plan. We will keep quiet about what we have learned until we find the original stone."

"It's probably been destroyed."

"What makes you think so?"

"Well, Dad, put yourself in Huddlebeck's place. What

would you do after the men you hired had got hold of the original Stone and substituted the phony? Would you take a chance on keeping the original where it might be found? Wouldn't you smash it up into small pieces as soon as you got the chance?"

"Your logic is good, Tom. You are quite right. Huddle-beck undoubtedly had that stone destroyed soon after it was taken from the truck. But there is a possibility that he did not get the Mandan Stone."

"What do you mean by that?" asked Tom.

Whiz Walton turned to Gates. "You had the original in your truck, didn't you?" he demanded.

Gates shrugged his shoulders. "That's what I thought. We drove to the Mandan village and talked to an Indian guy named Wahkee. He seemed to be in charge of things. He spoke a little English."

"I taught him," Hamilton Quest said.

"He had a stone all packed in a crate ready for us to move."

Tom's father nodded again. "I have," he said, "a great deal of confidence in Wahkee. As a matter of fact, we are blood brothers. Before I left his village, I told him not to let the Mandan Stone out of his possession."

"Well, he didn't follow your instructions," said Gates. "He gave it to me and Gleason without any argument."

"The fact that it was crated and ready for you makes

me think it is more than likely that you may have received a substitute."

"You mean," exclaimed Whiz Walton, "that you think the original Mandan Stone is still in the Mandan village?"

"Yes, Whiz, and well guarded by Wahkee and his people."

"In that case," went on the reporter, "the men who stopped the truck got a slab that was just as phony as the one that went to the University!"

"Probably," smiled Hamilton Quest, "it was even more phony."

"Golly," Tom said, "that makes things easy! You can get the original stone from Wahkee. When those professors examine that, they'll have to eat their words!"

"That's why I sent for you, Tom. I plan to go to the Mandan village. I thought you might like to go with me."

"You bet I would!"

"Gulliver is going."

"What about me?" demanded Whiz Walton. "You can't leave me out."

"I will be glad to have you, Whiz." The scientist looked at Gates. "As for you, Gates—"

Gates said, "Mr. Quest, I'm on your side. I've already told you to count me in if there's anything I can do to help you."

None of them knew it, but every word that had been spoken from the time Tom Quest first entered his father's cottage had been faithfully recorded by a highly efficient apparatus hidden in a barn a hundred yards away.

CHAPTER 7

Bedtime Snack

THOUGH THE COTTAGE had only two bedrooms, the builder had made provision for house guests by including a screened-in porch on one side. One folding cot had been set up and provided with blankets for Tom. There was ample room for two more cots, which Gulliver produced from a storeroom, so that Whiz Walton and Gates, the truck driver, might have a place to sleep.

When the sleeping porch was ready, Gulliver decided to make a slight change in the plans.

"Yo'," he said to Gates, "stay right on in my room. I aim to bunk on the porch with Tom an' Whiz."

"I don't like to do you out of your bed," objected Gates.

"Yo' ain't puttin' me out. I'm movin' because I want it that way."

The five were seated around a table in the kitchen for a bedtime snack. The afternoon had been spent in preparation for the long trip to the Red River country and the Mandan village. Camping gear had been brought from storage and inspected. Road maps had been checked and a route marked out.

Gulliver had spent two hours going through the contents of his medicine chest.

"She's cluttered," he had said. "I got lots o' stuff in here that can be throwed out."

He had emptied the chest and spread out the various articles in his room. Then he had replaced every item. There had been some doubt about some of the bottles and jars for which he had never found a use, but the big man could not bear to part with them, so they all had gone back into the chest.

It had been decided that Gulliver would go ahead in the jeep with Tom and Whiz Walton. Hamilton Quest would follow in his coupé and take Gates with him to share the driving.

"I think," Hamilton Quest said, pushing back his plate, "we can start by noon tomorrow."

"Suits me," muttered Gulliver.

"I—uh—" began Gates uneasily, "I didn't figure on takin' a trip."

"I know," smiled the explorer. "You're going to need

clothing as well as toilet articles and a few other things. I'll drive you into town in the morning and we'll get you equipped."

"There—uh—there's just one—"

"At my expense."

Gates looked relieved. "That's swell of you, Mr. Quest," he said. "I sure hope I can make it worth while."

"Stand up."

The others looked at Gulliver, who was eyeing the truck driver.

"Who—me?" queried Gates.

Gulliver nodded. "I been wonderin' about yo' ever since we decided to take yo' along. Now I got to find out. Stand up."

Gates obeyed with a bewildered expression in his face. He rose slowly and stood before Gulliver.

"'Bout six-two, ain't yo'?"

"And a half," added Gates.

Gulliver reached out with both hands and gripped Gates' thigh. He pressed hard with his thumbs.

"Solid," he muttered with a nod of approval. "Good muscle."

He stood and felt of the truck driver's stomach, then his chest and arms, in much the same way as an efficient housekeeper might inspect a melon in the grocery store.

"What's all this?" demanded Gates.

"They ain't no tellin' what we're likely to run up against in that there Mandan village. If it comes to fightin', I like to know the caliber o' my guns. There don't seem to be nothin' pulin' about yo'. I wonder if yo' got spirit." He paused, and then spoke in a lower voice as if he were thinking out loud. "Too bad yo' got that rap on the head. If it weren't for that, I could maybe try yo' out."

"Try me out?" repeated Gates. "What do you mean?"

Gulliver grinned. "We could maybe rough-an'-tumble on the lawn. Course, I'm some bigger'n yo', but I could git down on my knees an' hold one hand behind my back."

"Come on," invited Gates. "Don't let the cut on my head stand in your way. What's more, you'd better stand on both feet and use both hands. You'll need 'em!"

Gulliver's face contorted in a grin. "I guess yo' got spirit." He jabbed one fist playfully into the hard, flat stomach of the truckman, saying, "Sit down, Gates. Yo'll do."

Gates sat down smiling at the others, then turning to Gulliver, he said, "In case you're interested, I held the boxing championship of the Marine Corps a few years ago."

Gulliver nodded. "Me," he said, "I never done no boxin' in one o' them there rings."

"You didn't?"

"Yo're lookin' at my nose. I reckon yo' think I got that box-fightin', but that ain't the case. An ornery steer done that. The critter made me so doggoned frothy, I let fly with this here fist." Gulliver held up a balled fist, the size of a boxing glove. "I didn't stop to think that that there was a prize steer. I let him have it right between the eyes."

Gates grinned. "Then what did the steer do?" he asked.

"Him?" demanded Gulliver in surprise. "I just told yo' I hit him with all my strength. How could yo' expect the poor critter to do anythin' after that? Course I had to pay the owner for the damage, but it was worth it. I never et a better steak."

Tom Quest had been silent for some time.

"Is something bothering you, son?" asked his father.

The boy said, "I've been thinking."

"About what?"

"Blank cartridges."

"Them things!" put in Gulliver. "They was yo' dad's idea."

Tom looked at his big friend. "You said you were going to use them to scare away a prowler."

Gulliver nodded. "They was a critter coyotin' around durin' the night a couple o' times."

"Gulliver told me about him," Hamilton Quest said.

"He was going to sleep with his gun beneath his pillow and shoot if the man returned. I thought it might be someone from a near-by farm. I didn't want anyone to get hurt. I insisted that Gulliver load his gun with blanks which would serve to frighten anyone away."

"Who do you suppose it could have been?" asked Tom.

"I have no idea. However, he has not been back, so there is no use thinking about him."

"I'd like to git my hands on the snoopin' sidewinder," Gulliver said. "I'd unravel his spine."

"We will probably see no more of him," Hamilton Quest said.

But the explorer proved to be a poor prophet. The same mysterious prowler was at that very moment listening to the conversation and considering moves to checkmate the plan to secure the original Mandan Stone.

CHAPTER 8

The Talking Wire

GULLIVER got out of bed at daybreak and dressed silently. He picked up his heavy boots and carried them into the kitchen to be put on later.

As a cook, the big man was surprisingly neat and efficient. He lighted several burners in the stove and beneath the oven, and turned them to just the right degree of heat. He made a batch of biscuits and, while the oven heated, prepared pancake batter and put the griddle on the stove to warm. He started coffee and put small sausages on to cook slowly. The biscuits went into the oven to cook while he set the table.

Before the meal was ready, Hamilton Quest appeared in the doorway.

"Aw, gosh, Perfessor," said Gulliver. "Did I wake yo' up?"

"No," replied the other with a smile.

Gulliver said, "I figured to let yo' sleep until the last minute. Now I can put on my boots. I'll call the others."

With utter disregard for the peaceful sleep of anyone but Hamilton Quest, Gulliver clumped to the screened porch after pulling on his heavy boots, and wakened Tom and Whiz by the simple expedient of gripping each folding cot by the side and dumping the contents to the floor.

"What the sam hill—" began Whiz Walton angrily from a tangled mess of blankets on the floor.

"Git up, git up!" roared Gulliver. "Yo' aimin' to sleep all day?"

Tom picked himself up sleepily and rubbed his eyes. "What time is it?" he asked.

"Time to git gittin'!"

Fragrant aromas came from the kitchen. Whiz Walton sniffed audibly. "Nectar and ambrosia," he said. "Don't tell me I'm mistaken."

"Git geared for breakfast," replied Gulliver. "It's a fried egg sunny side up, toppin' a stack o' flapjacks soppin' up honey. They's also sausages an' toast with some jam made out o' wild strawberries."

"Oh my!" exclaimed the columnist, leaping to his feet and reaching for his clothing.

"Come an' git 'er, or I'll throw 'er out!" Gulliver

pivoted and strode to the bedroom that had, until the night before, been his. He slapped the closed door with his open hand in a way that fairly shook the house, then turned the knob and stuck his head inside.

"Yo', Gates!" Gulliver's voice at best was unmusical. When he pitched it above a conversational level, it had the nerve-jangling quality of a buzz saw striking a nail.

The covers on the bed seemed to explode. They flew ceilingward, and before they settled Gates was out of bed and standing in the middle of the floor with both fists swinging wildly. His eyes were still closed.

Gulliver stepped in and grabbed one of the fists in mid-air to stop a half-completed side-arm swing.

"Lay off!" he bellowed.

Gates opened his eyes, and for an instant his face was filled with panic. Then he relaxed and grinned. "Oh," he said, relieved, "it's you. Now I remember."

"Yo'," said Gulliver severely, "don't want to do no sittin'-up exercises in a room the size o' this. Yo're like to bust somethin'. Go outside if yo' want to spread yo' loop."

"Setting-up exercises my eye!" retorted the truck driver. "I thought I was back on a Pacific island dodging a Kamikaze plane." He looked around the room. "I couldn't have been dreaming," he continued. "What was that awful noise?"

"I didn't hear nothin'," said Gulliver. "I just tapped on yo' door, then called to tell yo' it was time to rise an' shine."

Soon after breakfast Gates drove into the business section of Lorraine with Whiz Walton and Tom's father. Gulliver sent Tom outside while he cleaned up the dishes and disposed of things that might spoil if left in the refrigerator for the duration of the trip to the Red River country. There were other details to which he had to attend in closing up the cottage, and Tom was free for at least an hour.

The trees surrounding the cottage had once been part of the wood lot of a farmstead. Tom made his way through them to explore the ruins of the old farmhouse itself, which had burned down many years before. The fireplace and chimney were still intact, rising nakedly above the rubble of stones and charred wood that lay half-covered by rank weeds.

Grass swished around Tom's knees as he crossed the clearing to the old gray barn that had defied the efforts of wind and storms to blow it down. Many of the wide boards that formed the siding hung askew, supported by a single nail, and there were many openings in the roof where the shingles had blown away.

Tom stood for a moment looking at the structure while trying to decide whether he should take the time to explore the inside. Then he saw the wire. It was so fine that it was almost imperceptible. It came out of the trees in the direction of the cottage and entered the barn through a small hole near the eaves.

Tom moved to the barn and stood directly beneath the wire where it entered the building. Close to the barn the soil had been washed away by water dripping from the roof. The ground was covered by bare stones. Two indentations about eighteen inches apart indicated that a ladder had been recently raised against the barn's side, and between the square depressions and the foundation of the building, Tom saw a number of chips—the kind that are formed when an auger is used.

Someone, Tom decided, very recently had drilled a hole in the barn so that the wire could be taken in.

"That settles it," he told himself, "I'm going inside and look around."

There was no door to cover the big square opening in the end of the barn that faced the highway. A number of birds flew from the rafters when Tom Quest stepped inside. The dirt floor was mottled by patches of sunlight that streamed through holes in the roof.

Halfway back, a perpendicular ladder connected the ground floor with the loft. Tom noted as he climbed the ladder that two of the cleats were new. The wood was white and the heads of the nails were shiny. This newness was in strange contrast to the rest of the tumble-down structure.

The loft was about a quarter filled with hay which had been pushed into a far corner. In another corner, the one nearest to his father's cottage, Tom saw a walled-off area. It seemed to have been built as a sort of storeroom, with a door that was held closed by a piece of strap iron resting in sockets.

The wide, warped boards of the floor creaked loudly beneath Tom's weight. He lifted the strap iron from the socket and swung open the door.

The room was about ten feet square. It was crudely finished, with a packing case to serve as a table and an inverted nail keg for a seat. The light was dim, but there was enough to show a complicated piece of electrical equipment on the packing case and close beside it an oil lamp.

Tom lighted the lamp and examined the machine. It was the latest and most efficient type of wire recorder, operated by dry-cell batteries. A wire ran from the machine upward to a newly drilled hole in the wall.

While Tom stood watching, there was a faint click and the spools of wire began to turn. Tom picked up one of the headphones and held it to his ear. The voice of Gulliver came through with crystal clarity.

"What time will yo' be back?" Gulliver was saying.

Then Tom heard his father's voice. "We still have considerable shopping to do, and Whiz wants to wait until the New York papers arrive, so we'll probably not be back for a couple of hours."

"That's all right," said Gulliver. "Me an' Tom will be ready when yo' come."

There was the click of a telephone being cradled, and the wire recorder stopped turning.

Tom remembered the prowler in the night. Whoever he was, his interest in Hamilton Quest was far more significant than the casual interest of a near-by farmer. Someone had gone to a great deal of pains to install a hidden microphone in the cottage, one so efficient that it picked up both ends of a telephone conversation and connected, by means of the thin wire, with the recording device.

"Gulliver's got to see this!" Tom told himself. He blew out the oil lamp and hurried back to the cottage.

CHAPTER 9

The Fat Man

IT DIDN'T TAKE LONG to find the microphone. It was a tiny instrument scarcely larger than a twenty-five-cent piece. It was fastened to the underside of Hamilton Quest's desk, close to the telephone. The wire followed the inside of the desk leg down through a tiny hole in the carpet and the floor.

With Gulliver holding a flashlight in the cellar of the cottage, Tom followed the wire along a stringer that supported the floor to a place where the wire went through a hole, and outside the house.

No one would be apt to see the wire outside unless he happened to be looking for it. It ran up the trunk of a tree close to the house, then right-angled through the leaves of other trees toward the barn a hundred yards away.

"I got it!" Gulliver exclaimed suddenly, snapping his fingers.

"What?" asked Tom.

"I been wonderin' how anyone could git inside the house to rig up that contraption. Yo' father hardly ever leaves the place, but yesterday he went in to the station to meet yo' an' Whiz Walton. Yo' remember he said he thought he locked the door?"

"That's right," replied the boy. "But the door was unlocked when we got back."

"An' Gates was inside. We figured Gleason must o' been the one that opened the door, but now I'm bettin' it was the critter that did this wirin' job. Maybe he was here when Gleason drove up in that there truck, an' had to scoot out fast so's he wouldn't be seen."

"That doesn't matter now," said Tom. "Come over to the barn and let me show you that recorder."

Gulliver stuck the flashlight into his hip pocket and said, "Let's git gittin'."

The old boards of the loft floor threatened to give way when Gulliver walked across them. Tom Quest lighted the oil lamp in the small enclosure, while Gulliver sprayed the light from his electric torch over the intricate mechanism resting on the packing case.

"This here," he said, "ain't in my line. How does she work?"

"I'll show you. We have a wire recorder at school," added Tom, "but it isn't as good as this one."

The boy touched a lever and two spools spun rapidly. They were about three inches in diameter and an inch in width.

"To start with," Tom explained, "the wire is on this spool. It runs through here," he pointed with his finger, "and it's wound on the other spool. Conversation or music or whatever you want to record is registered by magnetism, just as sound registers on a phonograph record by cutting a groove."

Gulliver rasped his heavy thumbnail across the stubble of beard on his chin. "Yo' mean," he said, pointing to the spinning spools, "that wire is takin' down what we're sayin'?"

Tom said, "No, it's not recording now. I just rewound some of the wire so we can listen to what has already been recorded." He pushed a button that stopped the spools of wire.

"Now," he said, leaning close to study the mechanism, "I'll see if I can make it operate. In this kind of a machine the action is automatic. It starts recording when sound comes through the microphone."

"How come yo' know all about it, Tom?"

"I read an article about this machine. It runs for about one minute after there is no sound, then it shuts off. It will keep going as long as anyone is talking in the house or wherever the microphones are placed."

The boy found a small switch that started the spools turning more slowly than before and in the opposite direction. Sounds came from the two headsets on the table. Tom picked one up, and Gulliver put on the other. Then they both listened.

Clearly recognizable was the voice of Gates telling about his experience on the highway when the truck had been halted.

Tom remembered that this conversation had taken place in the back bedroom, and admired the efficiency of the microphone that had picked it up from the living room. Every word was faithfully recorded.

Later the conversation in the kitchen during the bedtime snack came through the headphones, followed by the breakfast table talk.

Tom and Gulliver were so engrossed in listening that they did not hear the faint creak of floor boards in the loft. The man who moved as silently as possible was short and overweight. His face was round and flabby, and his stomach bulged. His features were small for so large a face. His mouth was almost lipless and his skin, though smooth, was too white to look healthy. In one pudgy hand he held a gun. It was a formidable weapon, a heavy-caliber pistol with a six-inch barrel.

He reached the open door unobserved by the huge man and the boy who listened at the wire recorder. Then, with the catlike grace that is sometimes found in fat men, he took one step forward, raised the gun, and brought it down with all his strength on the back of Gulliver's head.

Tom whirled quickly as Gulliver's knees buckled and the big man slumped to the floor.

"Don't move," the fat man said in a level voice.

Tom Quest looked directly into the barrel of the heavy gun.

CHAPTER 10

The Firetrap

Get back!" the fat man said, jabbing toward Tom with the gun. "Get back into the corner."

"Who are you?" Tom Quest demanded. "What's the idea of putting microphones in our house?" As he spoke Tom jerked off the headset and moved backward until the barn wall pressed against his shoulders.

In the yellow light of the oil lamp the fat man's face broke into a faint, mirthless smile. "I'm answering no questions," he said.

He shifted the gun to his left hand and, without taking his eyes off Tom, reached out and took both spools of wire from the recording machine. He dropped them into the side pocket of his coat, then backed to the door.

Tom Quest glanced at Gulliver, who lay motionless. The big man was on the floor between Tom and the fat man. Tom thought of charging but rejected the idea. He could hardly hope to dive across the room before that pudgy finger could tighten on the trigger.

The fat man was speaking. "The conversation in your father's cottage has been most enlightening." One more backward step carried him through the opening. He slammed the door, and then Tom heard the iron bar drop into place.

Tom's first concern was for Gulliver. Dropping quickly to his side, he removed the headset and examined Gulliver's head. There was a lump where the blow had fallen, but the skin was unbroken. Gulliver's pulse was steady and he was breathing regularly. Tom decided that his friend would regain consciousness shortly.

He rose and tried the door. It rattled loosely, but the iron bar on the other side was firm. Tom remembered that crude, but effective, fastening. The bar was about two inches wide and a quarter of an inch in thickness. It went completely across the door and rested in iron sockets which were bolted to the frame.

There was a faint chance that a hard blow would rip out the bolts. Tom drew back and threw his weight against the door. There was a resounding thud and a creaking, but the bar held firm.

He backed off and charged harder, using his shoulder as a battering ram. The flimsy walls of the building shook, but that was all that came of Tom Quest's effort.

Tom didn't notice that with each attack the oil lamp had been joggled closer to the edge of the crate on which it rested.

"Maybe I can do it," he muttered, "if I can get more of a running start."

He was breathless from his efforts and sweating profusedly. He bent and gripped Gulliver beneath the shoulders. He hauled the big man to the side so he could run the full length of the small room. He took a deep breath, gathered himself, and charged. There was room for only three or four steps, but with each step he gained momentum, and every ounce of strength in his strong legs went into the all-out effort.

When he hit the door a shock of pain stabbed through his shoulder. He felt the jar right down to his heels, and with it the sting of defeat. He knew, as he fell to the floor after the attack, that he had failed.

There was a crash of breaking glass. Tom looked up quickly and saw the danger instantly. The kerosene lamp had been jarred to the floor. It was smashed and the oil was spreading. Flames leaped from the center of the widening pool. In an instant all the oil would be in flames and then the barn itself.

Tom tore off his shirt as he bounded to his feet. He tried to beat out the flames, but only succeeded in fanning them to greater life. Fire licked at the flimsy crate and the bone-dry wall of the old barn. Tom's shirt was now afire. He threw it aside and turned to Gulliver.

The air was stifling. Tom gasped for breath as he dragged the big man farther from the flames. Gulliver stirred slightly.

"Gulliver! Gulliver!" choked Tom. "Wake up!" He shook Gulliver and slapped his cheeks.

"Wake up! Wake up, or it'll be too late!"

Gulliver opened his eyes, blinked a few times, and looked around stupidly. A crackling sound gave evidence that wood was burning. One wall of the barn was a sheet of flame that licked the ceiling.

"Wha—what hit me?" mumbled Gulliver. Then he saw the fire and the imminent danger shocked him into complete consciousness. He sat up quickly.

"We're trapped!" Tom said.

"The door!" boomed Gulliver, scrambling to his feet. "We got to git gittin'!"

"There's an iron bar across it. I tried to smash through, but I couldn't!"

"Lemme at it!" Gulliver threw his weight against the door with no more success than Tom had had.

"Stubborn, eh!" he bellowed. "Well, lemme git a runnin' start! I'll make that door jump out like a frog that sits down on an electric eel!"

He charged the length of the room, bellowing like an infuriated bull. There was a sharp crack as he hit the door and kept on going through the suddenly made opening, to spill with a clatter on the floor of the loft beyond.

"Yo', Tom!" he cried as he got to his feet, "what yo' waitin' for? Come on out o' that there firetrap!"

As a matter of fact, Tom was not waiting. He was out of the room almost as soon as Gulliver. He followed Gulliver down the ladder from the loft, and the two left the burning barn together.

Once outside, Tom raced to the telephone in his father's cottage, to call the fire department. Gulliver lingered to watch the flames, still wondering what had hit him.

CHAPTER 11

Westward Ho!

FLAMES fanned by a light breeze fed rapidly on the barn. In an incredibly short time the entire building was afire. Tom rejoined Gulliver, and as they watched from a safe distance, the boy told his friend about the fat man who had made off with the wire recording.

A small crowd assembled from the near-by farms and cottages. When the volunteer firemen saw that the barn was beyond all hope of saving, they remained to watch and wonder how the fire had started.

Tom Quest and Gulliver offered nothing to satisfy that curiosity. They thought it wiser to keep silent about the fat man and his wire recorder, at least until they had talked to Hamilton Quest.

Tom's father arrived with Lou Gates and Whiz Walton soon after the barn roof collapsed. They stayed until the danger of a grass fire was past, then all five returned to the cottage.

Tom told about the attack on Gulliver, the discovery of the wire recorder, and the other incidents preceding the conflagration. He gave a detailed description of the fat man.

Hamilton Quest shook his head slowly. "He is no one I know," he said.

Then Tom pointed out the tiny microphone concealed beneath his father's desk. A thorough investigation of the apparatus led to the discovery of other microphones in the cottage, all of which led to the fine wire strung through the trees.

"Did you tell anyone about the wire recorder?" Hamilton Quest asked.

The boy shook his head.

"How about you, Gulliver?"

Gulliver had been sitting in a corner of the room apart from the others, his eyes fixed on the floor and a sullen expression on his battered face. He felt humiliated and ashamed of the fact that a flabby fat man had been able to render him unconscious.

He looked up and shook his head. "Me," he said, "I didn't say nothin' to no one."

"Some of the people in the crowd," said Tom, "were wondering how the fire began."

"Let them wonder," Hamilton Quest replied. "The barn and the land on which it stood were taken by the state for taxes some time ago. No one stands to lose anything by the fire. If we tell the authorities about the fat man and the attack, we may be held here for days to answer questions, and I want to get started immediately for the Mandan country, especially if an enemy knows now that the real stone may still be there."

"I'm ag'in it."

Four pairs of eyes turned toward Gulliver.

"You're 'ag'in' what?" demanded Whiz Walton.

"Leavin'." For the first time the big fellow showed an interest in the proceedings. "That sidewinder that cracked me on the spire must be around here somewhere, an' I hanker to meet up with him an' square accounts."

"I'm sorry, Gulliver," said Hamilton Quest with a slow smile, "but you are overruled."

"Makes me so all-fired mad," grumbled Gulliver. "To think that he's likely the one who was coyotin' around here at night, an' me with blanks in my six gun!" He looked at Hamilton Quest accusingly. "Yo' made me put 'em in the gun!" he said. "If I'd o' had my way, I'd o' used a nine-gauge shotgun loaded with horseshoe nails an' rock salt."

"By the way," cut in Whiz Walton suddenly, "what about the wire running from this house to the ruins of the old barn? If the troopers find it, they may wonder what gives. Maybe we should take it down before we leave."

"I'll take it down," offered Tom Quest.

"Do that, son. Meanwhile, we will finish loading the cars and be ready to start as soon as you have finished."

It was a simple matter for Tom to climb the trees between the house and the barn and take down the wire, which had been lightly fastened with staples. He found a number of booster units designed to amplify the voices that had to be carried over the long extent of wire with sufficient volume to register on the delicate instrument.

When he had finished, and the house had been locked, he found the others waiting beside the two cars. He tossed the coil of wire and the boosters on the floor of Gulliver's jeep.

"We can throw them out somewhere along the highway," Tom said.

"If we find that fat man," rumbled Gulliver, "I'll ram 'em down his gullet!"

"Are we all set?" sang out Whiz Walton.

Gulliver stepped into the jeep, which listed heavily to the port side as he settled himself behind the steering wheel.

"Yo' seat," he said, jerking his thumb over his shoulder, "is waitin'."

Whiz Walton looked at the rear seat of the jeep, then

somewhat wistfully toward Hamilton Quest's snug coupé.

"Maybe," Gulliver said tauntingly, "yo're goin' soft. If yo' think the jeep is goin' to be too much for yo', yo' better ride with Tom's father an' Gates."

"Come on, Whiz," called Tom, "you're riding in the jeep with Gulliver and me."

The columnist suppressed a sigh as he thought of the long trip from the shore of Lake Erie to the Mandan territory beyond the state of Minnesota. But he was game. He climbed into the cramped quarters in the rear of the topless jeep, while Tom Quest took the seat in front at Gulliver's side.

"Yo' got the map, Tom?"

Tom nodded.

Gulliver's huge foot crushed the starter button. The unmuffled motor roared, then idled while Gulliver reached to the floor and brought up a pair of goggles which he handed to Tom Quest.

"Better put these on, Tom," he said. "When we git rollin', the wind gits kind o' lumpy."

"It would help if you'd put a windshield on this heap," Whiz Walton said.

"For what?" retorted Gulliver. "I like the wind. The chances are, before this trip is done yo'll git used to it, too."

"Not me," replied Whiz Walton.

Something in his voice made Gulliver turn to look. The reporter was grinning, and the grin was the only part of his face that could be seen. He wore huge goggles that covered not only his eyes but part of his nose and that part of his forehead that would have shown beneath his pulled-down hat.

"I've traveled with you before, Gulliver!" Whiz said. "I came prepared."

Gulliver glowered. "Maybe yo' came prepared for wind, but have yo' ever been up in that Mandan country?"

"Nope."

Gulliver chuckled. "Then don't yo' be so sure yo' came prepared!"

He jammed the accelerator to the floor and depressed the clutch. His little finger hooked the gearshift into low. The jeep shot forward, then tipped crazily as he twisted the wheel in a sharp turn to miss Hamilton Quest's car by a scant half-inch. There were two jolts as the front wheels, then the back, went through a ditch, and then a fast turn in the opposite direction by some miracle of manipulation brought the jeep on the highway, heading west.

CHAPTER 12

En Route

THE FIRST hundred miles were the hardest. After that Tom Quest and Whiz became accustomed to the steady rumble of the jeep's four-cylinder engine. Their faces became numb to the rushing wind and they acquired the knack of relaxing their muscles.

Tom had almost forgotten a lesson he had learned in Texas on the occasion of his first ride in Gulliver's jeep. To sit tense, trying to fight the bumps, would have been like landing stiff-legged on one's heels, whereas utter relaxation diminished the jars and jolts in just the same way that shock is taken out of a jump when one lands on the balls of his feet with knees flexed.

It was after dark when the jeep reached the outskirts of Chicago and stopped before a small, neat hotel. A motherly looking woman welcomed the travelers with a beaming smile and showed them to rooms that had been reserved in advance. It was an hour before Hamilton Quest arrived with Lou Gates.

All but Gulliver were well pleased with the hearty dinner that was served on a cool, screened-in porch. Gulliver complained that the food was lacking in "authority."

"I could fix 'er up," he said, "but I'd have to dig some stuff out o' the bottom o' my medicine chest, which same is in my jeep. I'll just eat for nourishment this time." He reached for the pepper and dusted the meat and mashed potatoes on his plate until Lou Gates gasped in dismay.

"Did yo' say somethin'?" Gulliver inquired.

Gates said, "You sure like pepper."

"This stuff," said Gulliver, holding up the pepper shaker, "don't amount to much. I use it just to give my palate somethin' to work on. When we set up a camp, I'll do the cookin'. Then I'll show you some downright lively eatin'."

Whiz Walton kept his eyes on his plate but winced inwardly at the recollection of his first experience with Gulliver's highly spiced concoctions. Gulliver had peppers and other condiments that came from some obscure source in Mexico. To a normal palate they were like a concentrated distillate of fire and brimstone.

Whiz Walton once, unknowingly, had taken a mouthful of food seasoned according to Gulliver's desires. It had fairly curdled his esophagus.

"I like lots of seasoning," commented Lou Gates.

"Brother," thought the reporter, "are you going to get it!"

Both cars were on the road at daybreak. Gulliver took the lead and drove through Chicago and the suburban communities. He stepped up the speed traveling north along Lake Michigan to Milwaukee. Then the route angled to the west, past countless lakes and wooded areas across Wisconsin.

The party camped that night in Minnesota. It was Gulliver who selected the campsite in a virgin forest off the highway. Aided by Tom and Whiz Walton, he unloaded the jeep while Lou Gates hauled a small tent, blankets, and a folding cot from the rear compartment of Hamilton Quest's car.

While Gulliver found and piled up a few stones to make a fireplace, and laid out supplies for the evening meal, Tom Quest and the newspaperman cut poles from near-by trees and set up the tent. Gates assembled a folding cot and placed it in the tent with blankets for the use of Hamilton Quest. The others, being younger, would have no trouble sleeping on the ground beneath the stars in sleeping bags.

Hamilton Quest stayed close to Gulliver and kept a watchful eye on supper preparations while he peeled potatoes and scraped raw carrots.

Without wasted effort, Gulliver prepared a batter of

flour, water, dried eggs, and a few other ingredients. He rolled this into one-foot lengths about a half-inch in diameter. Each length was then wrapped in a spiral around one end of a stick of green wood from which the bark had been removed. The sticks were arranged to hold the dough just over the glowing embers that had accumulated in the fireplace.

"The potatoes are peeled," announced Hamilton Quest as Gulliver fixed the last stick in position.

"Yo' slice 'em thin while I git the skillet hot, then keep an eye on my twists an' turn 'em frequent so they cook even all the way around."

The older man nodded. "You haven't made twists in a long time. They will taste good. Be a nice change from biscuits."

"I could," muttered Gulliver wistfully, "improve on 'em if yo' wasn't sittin' on my medicine chest."

"You know why I'm sitting here," replied Hamilton Quest.

Gulliver nodded. "The best o' my spices an' peppers are inside," he complained, slapping a thick steak on the skillet.

"That," said Quest firmly, "is where they are going to stay."

The steak sizzled violently for a moment, and when one side was thoroughly seared Gulliver flopped it in the pan.

"It's a doggone shame," he complained. "This here is a special steak an' I could make 'er downright fine, but I got nothin' to work with."

Hamilton Quest eyed the array of jars and bottles that he had permitted Gulliver to set out. "Salt, pepper, oil, vinegar, chili powder—" He enumerated several others, but Gulliver remained unenthused and went about his cooking as if he were wholly lacking in inspiration.

Thinly sliced potatoes were added to the skillet, then sliced carrots and onions. Gulliver brushed the top side of the steak with a special kind of vinegar, then oil. He sprinkled it with bits of thyme, rosemary, and several spices, and then some salt flavored with garlic. After a glance at his watch he turned the steak and repeated the seasoning.

The meal was served on tin plates and washed down with fresh milk that had been purchased during a stop for gasoline. Everyone pronounced the dinner excellent, and Lou Gates, sopping up steak gravy with bits of buttered twist, declared that Gulliver as a cook was even better than Smoky Joe.

Gulliver did not accept this remark as a compliment. He bristled. "Who's Smoky Joe?" he demanded.

"Runs a diner near Akron. All the truck drivers stop there. He serves a hamburger that's out of this world."

Gulliver's jaws worked mechanically and for some time he was silent, lost in deep thought. One could almost hear the clanking and grinding of his mental processes.

When the meal was finished he rolled up his sleeves and collected the tin plates and utensils.

"I'll help with the dishes!" Tom Quest offered.

Gulliver shook his head and jabbed toward Lou Gates with his thumb. "I want him to help."

"Me?" asked Gates.

"Pick up that there skillet an' follow me to the creek. While we're cleanin' things up, I want to ask yo' some questions about that there Smoky Joe an' his hamburgers."

"Now don't get sore, Gulliver. I didn't mean—"

"Yo' got me at a disadvantage. My wings was clipped. Tryin' to fix a meal with the boss sittin' on my special seasonin' is like tryin' to bulldog a steer with both hands tied behind yo' back."

"That steak you fixed," said Gates, "was as fine as anything I've ever eaten."

"Yo' like hamburgers."

"Sure thing, but—"

"Yo' come with me. We'll talk it over."

"Something," observed Whiz Walton as he eyed the two big men heading toward the near-by creek, "is stirring."

"What do you make of it, Whiz?" asked Tom, laughing.

The reporter shook his head. "I don't know, but I have a hunch that Gates is going to wish he'd never mentioned hamburgers."

Though the night was warm, Gulliver insisted on building up the fire so it would last until morning. Then he rearranged the sleeping bags, placing his own next to the fireplace, with Gates next in line. Whiz Walton's bag was next to the tent, and Tom crawled into the bag between Gates and the reporter.

The day had been a long one and everyone was tired. All were asleep soon after darkness fell.

Tom Quest didn't know how long he had been asleep. He opened his eyes in almost total darkness relieved only by a dim glow from the fireplace. He sniffed and realized what had awakened him. It was the tantalizing aroma of frying beefsteak.

Turning in his sleeping bag, he saw two bulky figures outlined against the firelight. Gulliver squatted before the fireplace and Lou Gates sat on the medicine chest. Tom could hear the whispered conversation.

"That sure smells good." It was Lou Gates' voice.

"Yo' ain't got much longer to wait," replied Gulliver. With a fork he speared something in the skillet and put it on a plate that rested on the ground close to the fire. He speared again and brought out a second huge hamburger patty which nearly covered the second plate.

"Like I told yo'," Gulliver said, "I couldn't use none o' my special seasonin' because Mr. Quest don't like it. But now things is different. These here hamburgers are goin' to get the works."

As he spoke, the big man glorified the hamburgers with the contents of a number of small jars that had not been used for the previous meal.

"Yo'," he continued, "git yo' fork ready an' be set for special eatin'. We got no rolls, but I reckon we won't need 'em."

Proudly Gulliver picked up one of the plates and offered it to Gates.

Tom Quest heard a stirring at his side, and then he heard Whiz Walton whispering, "This should be good!"

Tom turned and saw Whiz wide awake with his head propped up on one hand. "I must be a sadist," he murmured, "to let this happen."

"Here goes," said Gulliver, forking half of the patty on his plate. He chewed the mouthful with a rapt expression on his face.

Lou Gates said, "I'll see if you're as good as Smoky Joe." He put a massive chunk of meat into his mouth and started chewing. Then he stopped. He stopped with his mouth half open. His eyes opened wide and fairly spurted tears.

His plate moved slowly to the ground as if by its own weight. Gates had the lifeless, stupefied appearance that might come with the impact of a bolt of lightning. Then he regained control of his voice and muscles, and as if in sheer exuberance at the sudden release from total paralysis, every muscle moved at once. His head jerked back, he leaped to his feet, and his hands shot out before him like those of one who has been stricken blind and gropes in darkness.

The shrill cry of utter agony that split the night must have wakened every sleeping creature for miles around. The woods resounded with the frightened cries of birds, and a rustling of dry leaves on all sides gave evidence of countless small animals escaping from a world of terror.

Gulliver lowered his empty plate and offered a canteen to Gates. "I," he said placidly, "keep water handy in case there happens to be a sissy that don't like food with authority."

"Water! Water!" bellowed Gates, still groping with his hands.

"It's here," replied Gulliver calmly. "This canteen."

Gates couldn't see beyond the tears. Gulliver placed the two-gallon canteen in the reaching hands. He picked up what was left of Lou Gates' portion of the midnight snack.

"It'd be a shame to waste good eatin'," he observed.

He finished the hamburger in two huge bites while Gates let the cool water sluice his tortured mouth and throat.

Hamilton Quest appeared at the opening of the tent and demanded, "What's going on?"

"Nothin'," replied Gulliver innocently. "Me an' Lou Gates got a mite hungry, so I fixed him a hamburger—like he was braggin' he got at Smoky Joe's."

"Wow!" gasped Gates when he could speak. Then after a pause during which he apparently tried without success to think of a more fitting expression, he again said in a thin voice, "Wow!" and moved limply toward his sleeping bag.

CHAPTER 13

Explosion on the
Highway

AFTER THE MIDNIGHT EXPERIENCE with Gulliver's cooking, Lou Gates was a very subdued individual. At breakfast he complained that his throat was raw and sensitive, and he waited until his coffee was almost cold before drinking it.

As if to heckle the truck driver still further, Gulliver tossed aside the steaming contents of his tin cup, saying, "One thing I can't tolerate is cold coffee."

He refilled his cup from the pot that bubbled on the stone fireplace, and drank it scalding hot in a single gulp. He exhaled heavily. A cloud of steam issued from his mouth.

"That was better," he muttered complacently.

"Show-off," said Gates in a low voice. "But just wait, that's all."

Gulliver glanced at the truck driver. "What did yo' say?" he demanded.

"Maybe my throat isn't lined with asbestos, but you just wait," Gates retorted.

Gulliver grinned. "For what?"

"You'll see."

The others, seated around the fireplace in the early morning mist, sensed that a good-natured feud was growing between the two strong men, and anticipated interesting developments to come.

The two cars were loaded by sunrise. It was a long trip diagonally across the state of Minnesota, but it was not monotonous. There were countless bridges across small streams, and an almost continuous succession of lakes separated by great stands of virgin timber that had not yet known the devastating march of the lumber industry.

Tom took a turn at the wheel after the noonday stop, and slowed the pace so that they might better enjoy the interesting countryside.

Late afternoon brought the Red River into view.

"Tonight," sang out Whiz Walton, "we camp in North Dakota."

The crossing was made at Moorhead without incident. Tom turned into a gas station in Fargo on the North Dakota side of the river and stepped out to stretch his legs while the jeep's tank was being filled. A moment later, Lou Gates drove Hamilton Quest's car in and stopped at an adjacent pump.

Both cars were filled with gasoline and radiator water. The tires and batteries were checked and the oil was changed.

The truck driver, for the first time, showed particular interest in the vital parts of the jeep. While the hood was raised he poked around the small four-cylinder engine. Gulliver stood watching like a brood hen.

"Not much to it, is there?" Gates observed without looking up.

"They's enough," retorted Gulliver. "What more do yo' need?"

When Gates made no reply, he went on, "Lots o' these new cars got no end o' gadgets an' gimmicks to clutter up things. Them ramgudgeons just make it harder to git at the works when somethin' goes wrong."

"I didn't know," muttered Gates, "that you were a mechanic."

"Who says I am?" demanded Gulliver.

"You don't make your own repairs?"

"This here jeep don't need repairs. I feed 'er gas an' oil, an' let 'er rip."

After a short consultation it was decided to take advantage of the daylight that remained and cover as much ground as possible before camping for the night.

Hamilton Quest produced a map on which the route had been carefully drawn, and indicated the area surrounding the Mandan settlement. There were no roads, no cities, no labels of any sort in that area.

"The last part of the trip," Tom's father explained, "is going to be pretty rough. We will have to travel very slowly on old wagon roads, but I would like to reach the Indians tomorrow. We'll do it if we can cover another fifty or seventy-five miles before we camp tonight."

"We can cover more than that," said Tom. "We don't have to stop as soon as it gets dark."

"It would be difficult to find a good campsite in the darkness, Tom."

"That's so," agreed the boy.

"Follow the route for about seventy-five miles, then stop at the first likely campsite you find."

"I'll take 'er from here," said Gulliver. "Yo', Tom, take the other seat."

He slid behind the steering wheel and turned back to look at Gates, who was just entering the coupé.

"Yo', Gates!" he bellowed.

"What?"

"I'll show yo' what four cylinders can do. I'm settin' the pace. Yo' just try to keep up!"

With that, the big man tugged down his hat and kicked the starter.

"Hang on!" he cried to Whiz and Tom as the jeep took off with a jerk.

For twenty-five miles Gulliver held the throttle to the floor with one foot while he dangled the other foot over the side of the jeep as a gesture of nonchalance. The road ahead was absolutely straight for as far as one could see, and for some time there had been no traffic. Then a large truck appeared in the distance over a slight rise.

Tom Quest glanced at Gulliver, then back at the on-coming truck. There was ample room for passing. There was no reason for concern.

Gulliver swerved ever so slightly and brought the racing jeep to the right side of the highway. The driver of the truck, still far ahead, did the same. And then it happened.

The truck suddenly seemed to disappear in a ball of fire. Then the fire gave way to a cloud of smoke and the truck emerged zigzagging from one side of the highway to the other for a moment. Then it left the road entirely to bounce crazily across the ditch and into a tree.

All this happened before the dull *boom* of the explosion reached the ears of those in the jeep.

14

Dead Man's Tale

IT's ON FIRE!" shouted Whiz Walton as flames leaped from the hood of the wrecked truck.

"Get your feet out of the way!" cried Tom Quest. He stepped over the back of the front seat, clinging with one hand to keep from being thrown out of the rocketing jeep. "There's a fire extinguisher somewhere!" He crouched as the columnist pulled his long legs to one side, and pawed through the assortment of tools and camping gear on the cramped floor space.

"Hang on!" boomed Gulliver above the roaring engine. "We're cuttin' off the road to git there fast!"

Tom was thrown to one side by a sudden lurch as Gulliver turned to the left. The jeep took the ditch with all four wheels off the ground, then bounced and jounced across the field and came to an abrupt halt near the burning truck. Gulliver cut the ignition and was out of the jeep before the engine died.

"Tom!" he cried, "where at's that fire-foam gadget?"

"I have it!" Tom brought up a cylindrical tank to which was attached a length of hose that ended in a conical nozzle.

"Give it here!" shouted Gulliver, "an' yo' stay back!"

Tom passed the fire foam to the big man as Whiz Walton cried, "Holy mackerel! That truck—look at the name on the side!"

In yellow letters on the green side of the closed truck Tom Quest saw two names, "Gates and Gleason." The man in the cab appeared to be unconscious.

"We've got to get him out," said Tom.

There was a swishing sound and great billowing foam sprayed from the fire-fighting equipment in a white cloud that blanketed the smashed front of the heavy truck.

Tom Quest was only half aware of the fact that his father's car was bumping along to a halt beside the jeep. The boy raced to the door of the truck and pulled it open.

"I'll give you a hand," Whiz Walton said.

The driver was not only unconscious but obviously badly hurt. His head was cut in several places by glass from the shattered windshield, and the steering wheel seemed to have been jammed against his chest with crushing force. He slumped sideways as Tom Quest gripped his shoulders and eased him from the seat.

"I'll take his legs," said Whiz Walton, reaching.

"Let me help!" It was Gates who was calling as he approached on the run.

"We have him," replied Tom Quest.

Tom's father approached carrying a blanket which he spread on the ground. "Lay him on this."

Tom and the reporter lowered the unconscious man gently, then Tom said, "I'll get the medicine kit." He hurried toward the jeep.

Gulliver turned off the spray, then threw back the truck's bent hood to make sure no fire lingered underneath.

Hamilton Quest examined the injured driver expertly, then shook his gray head slowly.

"Here's the first-aid kit, Dad," Tom said.

"There is little we can do," replied his father.

"Do you mean he's dying?" Lou Gates asked in a shocked voice.

"His chest is crushed, and I am sure there are other internal injuries." Hamilton Quest wiped away the blood from the scalp wounds, then washed the man's face with cold water from the canteen.

"Isn't that your truck?" he asked.

Lou Gates said, "Yes, and you can guess who the man is."

"Gleason?"

"That's right." After a pause Gates spoke again. "Gosh!" he murmured in a low, awed voice, "I didn't expect him to go—like this."

"Did yo' see what happened?" demanded Gulliver.

"There was an explosion," put in Whiz Walton.

"We saw it," said Gates.

The columnist continued, "From where I sat, it looked as if someone had planted a bomb beneath the hood of the truck. The flames seemed to shoot out on all sides, then Gleason lost control."

"It was a bomb," Gulliver confirmed. "Yo' look at that truck an' yo' can see where it was planted down low beneath the floor boards where the clutch pedal goes through. That part o' the truck is blowed to smithereens."

There was a low moan from Gleason. His lips worked and his eyelids fluttered.

"Is he coming to?" asked Tom.

"Perhaps." Hamilton Quest again wiped the pale face with the cloth that had been dipped in cold water.

Gleason opened his eyes.

"Gleason," said Lou Gates, leaning close. "What happened?"

Gleason looked at his former partner for fully a minute before he spoke. "I—I—I got—what I asked for," he said in a faltering voice.

"What happened?"

Gleason's mouth twisted into a bitter smile. "Ambitious," he murmured. "I—" He was seized by a fit of coughing after which he closed his eyes as if he had no strength left to hold up the lids.

Then his eyes opened again and he reached up with one hand to clutch feebly at the sleeve of Lou Gates' shirt. "I'm—sorry, Lou—for double-crossing—"

"Don't worry about that now."

"I'm—I'm going, Gates. I know that. First—there's things I want—to tell." He paused and looked at the others, who were gathered close. His eyes moved slowly from Gulliver to Tom Quest, then to Tom's father.

"I hope," he said, looking at the older man, "you win."

Gleason clung doggedly to the slender thread of life while he told the story of the past few days. There were times when his voice was barely a whisper, and other times when his narrative was broken by long pauses during which he mustered strength to continue. His story filled in many gaps and confirmed some of the things that had been surmised.

He began with the day that Gates had determined to call on Hamilton Quest and make a clean breast of the fake holdup on the highway, when the hirelings of Hector Huddlebeck had stolen what they thought was the Mandan Stone, and substituted the rank imitation in its place.

Gleason had slugged Gates, then gone on to the cottage near Lorraine. He intended to negotiate with Hamilton Quest, to sell him information about the substitution of the stone. Driving the truck around to the rear, Gleason had tried the back door but found it securely locked. He had then walked around to the front, found the front door unlocked and the house empty.

Impulsively he had grasped what seemed to be a splendid opportunity to play for bigger stakes. Making sure he was unobserved, he had dragged his unconscious partner into the house. After a short prowl, he had found Gulliver's pistol, and cold-bloodedly shot at Lou Gates. When he left the house, he believed his partner was dead. He had fired at such close range that he had no doubt about the fatality. The possibility that the gun might be loaded with blanks had never entered his mind.

Later on, in Cleveland, he had called on a man named Morton, with whom he had made the original negotiations to pick up the stone in the Mandan village. There had been a fat man in Morton's office at the time. Morton had dismissed the fat man, telling him to wait outside.

Alone with Morton, Gleason said he had found Lou Gates murdered, and threatened to implicate both Morton and the head of the syndicate, Hector Huddlebeck himself. He demanded a substantial sum of money. Morton made vague promises and told Gleason to return in the afternoon.

It was not until later that Gleason learned the fat man had preceded him to Hamilton Quest's house that day, had picked the lock of the front door, and installed the hidden microphones connected to the wire recorder in the old barn. The fat man had just finished the installation of these microphones when he heard the Gates and Gleason truck pull up at the rear of the house. To avoid discovery, he had been compelled to make his escape through the front door, leaving it unlocked.

When Gleason returned to Morton's office later that afternoon, he was told to hold himself in readiness, and be prepared to start out with the truck at a moment's notice.

At this point in the narrative, Gleason's strength seemed to ebb rapidly. His breathing came in tortured gasps and his pulse was weak and ragged. He closed his eyes and for a time it seemed as though he were unconscious.

Hamilton Quest crushed a small ampoule and held it

close to Gleason's nostrils. The air was filled with a pene-
trating odor far stronger than spirits of ammonia.

Gleason shuddered and opened his eyes. "Al—most
through," he whispered. "Where—was I?"

Lou Gates said, "Morton told you to be ready for a
trip."

Gleason nodded almost imperceptibly. "He—called
me after supper. I—I brought the truck to his office. The
—fat man was there—and—half a dozen others—tough-
looking guys like—gangsters. They all carried guns. They
—climbed into the truck—and—so did the fat man and
Morton.

"We—we drove steady, taking turns—kept going
night and day to—Huddlebeck's place near the Mandan
village." Gleason looked at Gates. "I learned," he said,
"that you were still alive. I—I'm glad.

"Also found out—the fat man had learned that the
real stone was still in the Mandan village—got that from
the—wire recorder." Another coughing spell left Gleason
too weak to continue.

"What happened after you got to the village?" asked
Hamilton Quest.

Gleason's lips moved, but no sound came from them.

"Did they tell you to go back to Cleveland?"

The dying man nodded. "Fixed—fixed the truck," he

whispered. "Planted time bomb—know it now—they wanted to g-get me out of the way."

He spoke no more. The sound of a siren came from the near-by highway, and a police car screeched to a stop next to Gulliver's jeep.

"This man," Hamilton Quest said, rising to meet the officers, "is dead."

CHAPTER 15

The Last Leg

"ORDINARILY I do not believe in withholding information from the law," said Hamilton Quest.

"What them lawmen don't know won't bother 'em," Gulliver declared. "What's more important, the cops won't bother us."

Tom Quest said, "You answered all their questions, Dad. You told them how we saw the truck go off the highway, smash into the tree, and burst into flame."

Hamilton Quest nodded slowly. "Someone," he said, "fixed a timed explosive charge beneath the engine of that truck to kill Gleason. It was premeditated murder. There is no doubt of that."

A great deal of time had been lost at the scene of the smashup. One of the police officers had gone to the nearest telephone to make arrangements for the coroner to come from the county seat. Another officer had taken statements.

Hamilton Quest and the others answered all the questions without elaboration. Tom's father had done most of the talking, and taking their cue from him, no one said that the explosion actually was evidence of murder. Nor did they mention the fact that Lou Gates was part owner of the wrecked truck, and a former partner of the dead man.

Camp had been made about ten miles beyond the scene of the disaster. All five of the travelers gathered in the small tent to discuss events by the light of a gasoline lamp.

Tom and his father sat on the bunk, facing Gulliver and Lou Gates, who were on the ground with their knees drawn up. Whiz Walton was perched on a wooden chest that held some of Hamilton Quest's equipment. For some time Whiz had been writing in a notebook.

"I think," Hamilton Quest said, "the situation justified what we did. Or rather," he added with a slight smile, "what we did not do. If we had told about the time bomb and about our suspicions, and Gates' association with Gleason, we would have been taken for questioning. We might have been delayed for many days."

"That ain't all," put in Gulliver. "Them lawmen would o' barged up to the Huddlebeck layout an' made a general mess o' things without gittin' nowhere. Yo' done the right thing."

Gates had been acting rather subdued since the death of Gleason. Now he spoke in a low voice. "When they begin checking that truck," he said, "they'll find that I'm one of the owners. They'll probably be looking for me in Cleveland."

"They won't find yo' in Cleveland," grinned Gulliver. "Hey, listen!"

The other four turned toward Whiz Walton.

"I've been setting down the things that happened. Gleason filled in a lot of the gaps. I think I have everything in chronological order. Want me to give you a rundown?"

The columnist didn't wait for a reply. Looking at his notebook, he said, "Huddlebeck had to know what Mr. Quest would do after learning that the University professors found that hunk of stone to be a fake, so he sent the fat man to snoop around.

"The fat man may or may not have known that Gulliver was laying for him. At any rate, he decided to install microphones in the house and a wire recorder in that old barn. He waited for his chance to get inside the house when it was empty."

"And it came while I was in town to meet the train," put in Hamilton Quest.

"That's right. And before Gulliver got back from the University. Meanwhile, Gates and Gleason had disagreed and Gates had decided to go to see Mr. Quest.

"The fat man was in the house when they reached there. He saw the truck approaching; went out the front door, leaving it unlocked. Gleason had slugged Gates in the truck. He dragged him into the house and shot him —or thought he shot him.

"After all of us arrived at the cottage, the fat man got an earful. Among other things, he learned that the stone the Mandan Indians had turned over to the truck drivers probably was just as phony as the one that Gulliver brought back from the University."

Hamilton Quest nodded. "I'm sure of that now," he said. "Wahkee would die before he would break his promise to me, and he promised to hang on to the Mandan Stone."

The columnist continued. "As soon as the fat man reported that Wahkee still had the stone, it was decided to send a gang to the Mandan village to get it. Meanwhile, Gleason had tried to blackmail Huddlebeck's man, Morton. But they knew all about the attempted murder and Gleason was called back to furnish transportation for the gang."

"That was the evening of the day we found Lou Gates," Tom Quest said.

"That's right, Tom. The fat man caught you in the barn the next day. The barn burned down and it wasn't until two or three hours later that we set out from the cottage. As I dope it out, the Huddlebeck mob, all but the fat man, started the trip the night before. They got to the Mandan country well ahead of us because they didn't stop at night.

"Then they were through with Gleason and decided to get him out of the way."

"The dirty rats!" said Lou Gates. "They didn't have to kill him!"

"Yes, they did, Lou," Whiz said soberly. "He knew too much."

"We'll catch up to them polecats," promised Gulliver. "Just about the time the cops git around to learnin' that there was an explosion in the truck, we'll have our hands on the sidewinders that done it."

Whiz Walton closed his notebook with a snap. "I guess that summarizes it."

"I wonder," Hamilton Quest said slowly and with great concern, "what those hoodlums will do—or have already done."

Tom looked up quickly. "What do you mean, Dad?"

"They knew from the recorded information that Wahkee was still in possession of the stone, which will deprive Huddlebeck of very valuable property. The fact

that they murdered Gleason indicates that they are prepared to stop at nothing to get the stone. Moreover,
Wahkee wouldn't be able to fool them a second time."

"I wouldn't be too sure o' that," said Gulliver. "I've
known redskins that were downright clever."

"You forget, Gulliver, Huddlebeck's men know now
how to identify the stone. They know I scratched a tiny
spiral in one corner on the reverse side."

"Doggone," muttered the big man, "I had forgot yo'
made mention o' that while the recordin' gadget was
takin' down everythin' we said."

"I am worried about Wahkee. I wish—" Tom's father
left the sentence suspended.

After a pause the boy said, "What do you wish, Dad?"

"Never mind, Tom."

"Why don't we break camp right now and shove on?"
Tom exclaimed.

"Yo' mean that, Tom?" asked Gulliver.

"Why not? We have good spotlights on the cars. We
can find the road all right. If we reach the Mandans in
the morning instead of the afternoon, it might mean the
difference between life or death to Wahkee."

"How about you, Whiz?"

"I'm all for it!"

"Me, too," chimed in Gulliver, getting to his feet. He
looked at Hamilton Quest and said, "How about it?"

The older man nodded. "I would much rather go on instead of spending the night in camp."

"That does it!" Gulliver grabbed one end of the bunk. To Tom and his father, he said, "Yo' two goin' to stand up? Or should I fold up this bunk with yo' inside it?"

As the two arose, he turned to Gates. "Go pack the cookin' gear while I stow the tent."

In less than thirty minutes the two cars rolled from the campsite to the dirt road, and a newly installed spotlight on the jeep pencilled into the night beyond the twin beams of the headlights. Lou Gates followed closely at the wheel of the coupé.

CHAPTER 16

The Mandan
Village

THE TWO CARS moved at a steady pace through the night. Tom Quest and Whiz Walton huddled low in the open jeep and pulled their jacket collars tight around their throats in an effort to combat the night chill. The sky was overcast at daybreak. A cold gray mist hugged the ground and fogged the landscape. The map spread out on Tom's knees was limp with moisture.

"We gittin' close?" rasped Gulliver.

"As nearly as I can figure from this map, we're nearly there."

"How near?" demanded Whiz Walton, leaning forward to eye the map over Tom Quest's shoulder.

"We crossed a stream a few minutes ago." Tom

pointed to a snaky line on the map that cut the route at right angles. "If this was the stream we crossed, we should be within sight of the Mandan village almost any minute."

The road had been built through a dense stand of big timber, and the men who had built it must have despised straight lines. It meandered like a stream in level pasture-land.

Gulliver's patience was worn paper thin. While he steered the jeep first one way, then the other, he relieved his feelings by a constant grumble of contempt for the builders of the roadway. At one point he expressed a fervent hope that he might someday drive that way at the controls of a twenty-ton bulldozer.

"Then, by thunderation, I'd straighten out this road!"

The woods ended. A quarter of a mile ahead, they could see the houses of the Mandan Indians huddled on a vast expanse of open plain. The houses were alike in shape and style and were set close together in a large circle. They were circular in shape and varied in size from forty to sixty feet in diameter. The domed roofs gave them the general appearance of huge Eskimo igloos.

Tom was somewhat surprised to see that the dwellings were just as he had visualized them from his father's description. He recalled the details of construction. Timbers about eight inches in diameter and six feet in height were placed on end to form a solid circular wall. On top of these, other timbers of the same width but twenty or twenty-five feet long were placed at an angle of forty-five degrees so that they slanted toward the apex and formed the roof of the lodge. These timbers were supported by long poles from the floor. The roof was covered with a mat of willow boughs, then the entire lodge, walls and roof, was coated with a two-foot thickness of hard, tough clay which was impervious to water. Hamilton Quest had said that from twenty to forty people, all members of a single family, occupied a lodge.

Gulliver brought the jeep to a halt a few yards from the nearest lodge, and Lou Gates drew the coupé alongside.

There was no sign of life in the Mandan village. And this was strange, because the Mandans were a curious people. The unmuffled engine of the jeep should have been a signal for every man, woman, and child to come on the run to investigate.

Gulliver reached behind his seat and found his favorite gun and gun belt. He stepped out and buckled on the hardware.

"What d'yo' make of it?" he asked as Hamilton Quest came from the other car.

"I don't know."

"This ain't the welcome I figured on."

"Nor I."

"We goin' to wait here an' see what happens, or go an' rouse up some o' them redskins?"

"The houses seem to be occupied," Hamilton Quest said as he noted the smoke of cooking fires rising from the vent holes in the roofs.

"Was it like this the last time you came here, Dad?" asked Tom.

"No, it was not at all like this."

"Which one o' them overgrowed toadstools is Wah-kee's?" asked Gulliver.

"Wahkee is the chief. He lives—at least he did live—in *that* house."

The explorer pointed to a lodge much larger than the others, in the front of which the pelt of a white buffalo was suspended like a flag at the top of a long pole.

The fronts of all the dwellings faced an open circular space about a hundred and fifty feet in diameter, which Tom's father said was used for public games, festivals, and religious ceremonies. In the center of this area stood an object of great religious veneration. Standing eight or ten feet high, it was made of planks held together by hoops in the form of a large barrel. It held the "Medicine" of the Indians.

Wahkee's lodge was on the far side of the circle.

Gulliver hitched up his belt. "What're we waitin' for?"

he demanded impatiently. "Let's go an' find Wahkee an' see what's doin'."

"Someone," Tom cried out suddenly, "is coming from his lodge! Two people, in fact!"

The first was tall and thin. The other, one pace in the rear, was short and fat. They wore deerskin tunics that came nearly to the knees and leggings that were tightly fitted to the leg. Their moccasins were made of buckskin.

The tunic and the leggings were elaborately ornamented with bits of fur and porcupine quills. Both men wore picturesque headdresses made of raven's quills and ermine, and the thin man's hair was long, hanging below the shoulders. This man, who walked ahead, wore the horns of a buffalo attached to the top of his headdress on each side.

"Dad," said Tom, "you told me that only a chief of great renown was allowed to wear horns on his headdress."

"That's right, Tom."

"Is that lean galoot Wahkee?" asked Gulliver.

"No. That is Wahkee's father."

"Yo' know him?"

Hamilton Quest nodded soberly. "He is very old. He was the chief for many years. He had relinquished his position in favor of his son Wahkee. Now he again is wearing the headdress of horns. I wonder what has happened to Wahkee."

"Who's the other critter?"

"I don't know, Gulliver. I don't remember seeing him the last time I was here."

"Do you know the name of Wahkee's father?" asked Tom Quest.

"He is called War-rah-pa. It means 'The Beaver.' I'd better go to meet him."

While the others waited, Hamilton Quest crossed the clearing to meet War-rah-pa. After a short conversation, he signaled for the others to come.

"We are invited to have breakfast in War-rah-pa's lodge," he explained.

"Did he say where Wahkee is?" asked Tom.

"No."

"Did he," demanded Gulliver, "tell yo' why all these other critters are stayin' out o' sight like we was a small-pox epidemic?"

Quest shook his head. "I think he will answer some of our questions at breakfast."

CHAPTER 17

The Sign of the Spiral

INSIDE THE LODGE it was hard to believe that time had not turned back a hundred years or more. On all sides there was evidence that the Mandans were content with their primitive methods of cooking, primitive tools and weapons, and their primitive way of life. Flat slabs of rock had been set into the dirt to form a floor which was swept very clean.

In the center of the floor, immediately under the skylight or air vent in the roof, was a circular hole about five feet in diameter and a foot in depth. A fire burned in the center of this depression beneath a kettle suspended from a tripod and filled with some kind of meat.

Close to the wall on all sides were a number of beds made of round poles lashed together, over which buffalo skins were stretched, with the fur side uppermost, about two feet from the floor. Close to the fireplace, buffalo robes and mats of rushes were spread on the floor.

The walls were decorated with shields and weapons. There were seven-foot spears tipped with stone, and many bows and arrows. Eagle feathers, tufts of fur, and porcupine quills were lavishly used, and there were many paintings of animals on the wall itself.

Two old women with snow-white hair were busy at the fireplace when Tom Quest and the others entered. War-rah-pa pointed to mats near the fireplace and invited his guests to be seated.

Gulliver sniffed, close to the kettle. "Whatever is cookin' in there," he said, "smells downright good."

War-rah-pa favored the big man with a slow smile. "You like?"

Gulliver's eyes widened. "Yo' savvy English?"

"Me War-rah-pa. Me father of Wahkee." The Indian placed his hand on the arm of Hamilton Quest. "Good friend," he finished.

Gulliver pointed to the short, fat Indian. "Who's he?"

"Him medicine man."

The short man turned and moved to one of the bunks near the wall where he lay down silently.

"What about Wahkee?" asked Whiz Walton. "And why is everyone in this village staying out of sight?"

Hamilton Quest said, "I will see what I can learn." He spoke in the native tongue and War-rah-pa replied. The conversation continued for some time while the women served a hearty meal of pemmican and buffalo ribs.

There was a kind of bread made out of corn with marrow fat in place of butter. The meal was served on dishes made of polished wood and eaten with spoons of buffalo horn.

War-rah-pa, in accordance with custom, did not eat with his guests, but supervised the serving of the meal and all the while continued his conversation with Hamilton Quest.

Gulliver ate heartily, chewing the tough, unsalted meat vigorously. Tom and Whiz Walton were not enthused about the fare, but managed to eat something. Lou Gates, sitting next to Gulliver, took a big mouthful of pemmican and made a wry face at the dried lean meat, which had been pounded fine.

"Yo'," said Gulliver, "eat what's on yo' plate. Eat it if it kills yo'. It won't do to offend these critters."

Hamilton Quest, who had become accustomed to the Indian food during his previous visit, had no difficulty.

"I'd give a lot to know what they're talking about," Whiz Walton observed with a slight nod toward the opposite side of the fireplace, where War-rah-pa and Hamilton Quest sat talking.

"So would I," replied Tom Quest. "Dad will tell us as soon as he gets a chance."

When the women had collected the empty plates, War-rah-pa rose to his feet and picked up the buffalo mat on which he had been seated. With great deliberation he turned it over so that the furry side was on the flagstone floor.

The inside of the skin was covered with gaudily colored pictures which represented animals, the sun and the moon, and Mandan spirits.

At one side of the pelt there was a figure that caught and held Tom Quest's attention. It was a spiral figure like the pattern on his ring, and beneath it were several words of Mandan.

Hamilton Quest looked at the words and then at War-rah-pa. The eyes of the two men met and exchanged a knowing look. War-rah-pa smiled and Hamilton Quest's head moved in a barely perceptible nod.

Whiz Walton was fairly trembling with eagerness. "There's something cooking here," he whispered to Tom, "and it's not buffalo meat!"

Hamilton Quest was speaking in English. "We would like," he said, "to pay our respects to the dead as soon as possible."

War-rah-pa nodded and said, "Is good."

"If it's all the same to you, Mr. Quest," Whiz Walton

said, "is not good. I can think of a lot of things I'd rather do. It—"

"It," cut in the explorer firmly, "is not all the same to me."

"Yo' mean," said Gulliver, "we got to go?"

"Yes."

"I don't git it."

"You will."

Gulliver frowned darkly. "I figured on spendin' some time goin' over my jeep, an' unpackin' some o' my gear."

"We will not need to unpack any equipment, Gulliver," said Hamilton Quest in a milder voice. "This lodge is to be at our disposal. We are to live here while we are in the village. As for the cars, they can stay right where they are."

He stood. "If the rest of you are through eating, we shall go at once to the Place-of-the-Dead."

18

The Jeep Sounds Off

THE PLACE-OF-THE-DEAD was separated from the village by a wall of wooden timbers set into the ground.

"I brought you here," explained Hamilton Quest, "so we could talk without being overheard."

It was a strange place, and it gave Tom an eerie feeling.

When a person dies in the Mandan village, the customary honors and condolences are paid to his remains. Then the body is wrapped tightly in a fresh buffalo skin and taken to the Place-of-the-Dead, where it is placed on a scaffold. The scaffold is made of four upright posts on the top of which are poles connecting the end posts. Willow boughs are laid across these poles to support the body above the reach of animals.

When the scaffold decays and falls, the nearest relatives bury all but the skull, which by this time has been bleached by the sun. The skulls are arranged in circles of a hundred or more and are protected and preserved as objects of veneration.

There were over a hundred scaffolds in straight lines on the level plain and, near by, several circles made of human skulls.

"What were you and the old chief talking about?" Whiz Walton asked Hamilton Quest.

"About Wahkee."

"Where is he?"

"I will tell you what War-rah-pa told me, and you can draw your own conclusions. The day before yesterday, Wahkee went hunting. He did not return. At sundown a strange Indian, a medicine man from another tribe, came to Wahkee's father, carrying the headdress of Chief Wahkee."

"You mean the cap with the buffalo horns that old War-rah-pa is wearing?" asked Tom.

"Yes, son. And there was a message from Wahkee. The young chief asked that his father take charge of the village until he returned. And Wahkee said the messenger was to remain in the lodge of the chief with strong medicine that would protect the village."

"He must be that round-bellied Injun."

Hamilton Quest said, "That's right, Gulliver."

"If it comes to a showdown o' magic medicine, I

reckon we can show rolypoly a few tricks. Recollect the time we was in Ecuador? Some o' my white man's magic made those head-hunters bug-eyed!"

"Keep still, Gulliver, and let Mr. Quest finish!" said Whiz Walton impatiently. "What do you make of it?" he went on, turning to the older man. "Do you think Wahkee was captured by the Huddlebeck outfit?"

"I think he was. I think they are holding him to make him tell where he hid the Mandan Stone."

"Where at is this Huddlebeck outfit? Did the old chief tell yo' that?"

"Yes, Gulliver. It is less than two miles from here due south through the woods."

"Then what're we waitin' for? I got some extra shootin' irons in my medicine chest. Let's strap on the hardware an' call on Huddlebeck or whoever's in charge o' his outfit, an' tell 'em we come to git Wahkee."

Lou Gates spoke. "Wait a minute, Gulliver. Mr. Quest hasn't finished."

"The medicine man had the old chief call all the people of the village together last night," Tom's father said. "He told them white men were on the way and that the white men would bring evil to the village. I don't know what else he told them, but it was enough to keep them in their lodges when we arrived. I think War-rah-pa is afraid of the medicine man."

"I'll bet he's a spy!" broke in Tom Quest.

"A spy?"

"Yes, Dad. I'll bet he's working for Huddlebeck and he's here to see that the old chief follows orders."

"That's possible."

Tom spoke again. "When War-rah-pa turned that buffalo hide over, he made it a point to show us that sign of the spiral. What did that mean?"

"It was a message from Wahkee. He put it there soon after he hid the Mandan Stone."

"Does it tell where the stone is hidden?"

"No, Tom. Freely translated, the message beneath the spiral meant, 'I have kept my promise.' "

"Is that all?"

Hamilton Quest nodded and said, "That's all. Wahkee made just one promise to me. He promised to protect the stone."

Gulliver shifted his weight uneasily from one foot to the other. He hiked up his trousers and scratched his chin. Finally he grumbled, "We're wastin' time. Wahkee knows where at that stone is hid. All we got to do is git Wahkee."

"You are right, Gulliver, but it won't do to go to Huddlebeck's headquarters wearing guns and looking for a fight. Remember what Gleason told us before he died."

"What was that?"

"A truckload of hoodlums came up here from Cleveland to help Huddlebeck."

"What of it?" retorted Gulliver, bristling. "It was just one truckload. Me an' Gates can likely handle 'em between us."

"Well, you are not going to try it."

"Aw-w-w, thunderation!" Gulliver's face assumed the sulking expression of a schoolboy. "What are we goin' to do?" he asked.

Before Hamilton Quest could reply, a raucous sound came from beyond the circle of houses. The effect on Gulliver was electric.

"That," the big man bellowed, "is my jeep! Someone's a-honkin' on the horn!"

There was a series of short bursts of the horn, followed by a long sustained sound.

"I'll teach someone a lesson!" roared Gulliver. He set out on the run with Lou Gates at his heels.

"Come on, Whiz!" Tom Quest cried. "We better go along!"

Hamilton Quest followed at a slower pace.

Gulliver reached the circle of lodges with Lou Gates close behind. Tom passed Gates in the race across the council ring and ran easily at Gulliver's side. Whiz Walton, shorter-winded than the others, had fallen behind.

Gulliver saw his jeep when he and Tom passed between two of the lodges on the far side of the circle, and bellowed like a wild bull at a man who had the effrontery to be occupying the driver's seat.

Gulliver completed the distance to the jeep and, without breaking his stride, stepped on the bumper, then the hood. Both hands shot over his head and slammed down on the shoulders of a white man who wore a red-and-black checked lumberjack shirt.

"Yo'!" shouted Gulliver. "Git out o' my jeep!"

He gave the other no chance to comply with the command. Still gripping the shirt by the shoulders, Gulliver leaped from the hood of the car to the ground and dragged the stranger out head foremost.

Tom Quest had rarely seen his big friend in such a rage.

"Wait a minute, Gulliver!" he said hurriedly. "The man didn't do any harm!"

"Honkin' my horn!" accused Gulliver. "Runnin' down my battery!"

He released his hold on the startled man and held one huge balled fist within an inch of his nose.

"For two cents, I'd ram this down yo' throat!" he threatened, shaking his fist. "I'd make yo' eat yo' teeth an' swaller 'em without no chewin'!"

Lou Gates arrived puffing, and Whiz Walton was covering the last few yards.

"What's up, Gulliver?" the columnist called.

"That's what I aim to find out!"

Tom Quest said, "Why don't you give the man a chance to speak?"

Gulliver stepped back. The stranger adjusted his shirt and regained a measure of composure. He was a well-built man of middle age and medium height. His face was tanned, but it was the tan of a sportsman, not the weather-beaten, leathery appearance of a man who spends all of his time in the open. His hair was partly gray, with a part low on one side. He had a heavy chin and a prominent nose. His eyes and mouth were narrow and hard. It was the face of a man who could be cruel and ruthless.

Tom noticed that he wore an expensive watch on his left wrist and a ring with a large diamond on one finger.

"I'm waitin'," Gulliver said. "Why'd yo' coyote around my jeep?"

The other spoke in a firm, clipped voice. "Because I wanted to talk to a member of your party."

"Yo' can talk to me. I'm Gulliver."

"I want to speak to Hamilton Quest."

"That's my father," Tom said. "He's coming now."

Gulliver still wore a belligerent expression. "First," he said, "yo' talk to me an' tell me what yo' want an' who yo' are."

"I'll tell you who I am. I'm Hector Huddlebeck."

Tom Quest was watching Gulliver's face. It changed expression just as Huddlebeck introduced himself. The black rage and fury disappeared. Gulliver's eyes widened and his chin became slack and dropped so far that his mouth was half open. It was an expression of incredulity Tom had never seen on Gulliver before. For once, the big man seemed to be at a loss for words.

Gulliver was looking past Huddlebeck toward the rear of the jeep. Tom turned his eyes in that direction and saw what seemed to be a nightmare come to life.

It stood on spindly bowlegs encased in doeskin and had the arms and torso of a stooped, bent-over old man. But the narrow shoulders were topped by the huge shaggy head of a buffalo, and perched between the horns was a raven.

As Tom stared, he heard Whiz Walton cry out, "Holy mackerel! What is that?"

Gulliver tried to speak but managed nothing more than an incredulous grunt.

Gates said in an awed whisper, "No! I don't believe it!"

CHAPTER 19

Hector Huddlebeck

A CACKLING LAUGH issued from somewhere inside the buffalo head. Then two skinny arms reached up and lifted the skull and the raven fastened between its horns, and it became evident that the apparition was simply an old Indian with an exceptionally elaborate headdress.

His face was a mass of wrinkles. He had no teeth and his mouth was so sunken in that his pointed chin almost touched the end of his oversized nose. He was grinning delightedly at Gulliver.

"Great day!" exclaimed the big man, eyeing the little Indian from head to toe. "Yo're better lookin' with yo' face inside o' that buffalo head."

The Indian stepped forward on his bowlegs and pushed past Hector Huddlebeck. He stopped in front of Gulliver and pointed to the jeep.

"Good medicine," he said. He pointed to Gulliver and repeated the expression, then slapped his own chest. "Me good medicine, too. Me great medicine."

His movements were quick and birdlike. Before Gulliver could object, he grasped the big man's hand and pressed something round and flat into the palm. He gave a cackling laugh, then turned and fled.

Gulliver looked at the object in his hand. It was a pocket mirror about the size of a silver dollar, the kind that had advertising on the celluloid back. Gulliver turned it over and read aloud: "Use Pear's Soap for Beauty."

Tom and Whiz exploded into guffaws.

"Don't underestimate that little fellow." It was the voice of Hamilton Quest, who had approached unnoticed.

Gulliver turned. "Who is he? Do yo' know him?"

"Yes. His name is Mah-to. He is the oldest Indian in the village, and until recently he was the most important and the most powerful."

"That bowlegged little galoot *important?*" asked Gulliver incredulously.

"He is the medicine man."

Gulliver held out the mirror on the palm of his hand. "He gave me this," he said.

"He has taken a fancy to you, Gulliver."

Whiz Walton spoke in a dry voice. "Do you think he loves you for yourself alone, or because you own a jeep?"

Huddlebeck broke in. "Are you Hamilton Quest?" he asked.

Quest lifted his eyebrows.

Tom said quickly, "Dad, this is Mr. Huddlebeck."

Huddlebeck struck a pose of genial good fellowship and extended his right hand. "Glad to know you, Quest," he said heartily. "Mighty glad. I've heard a lot about you."

"And I," Hamilton Quest said, "have heard about you. I suppose you have met my son and my friends."

"No, I haven't."

Introductions were made with strained formality. Tom, Whiz, and Gulliver were introduced, and then Lou Gates.

"Your name is familiar," said Huddlebeck.

Lou Gates nodded and said shortly, "It should be. My partner and I did a job for you. His name was Gleason."

A barely perceptible change of expression crossed Huddlebeck's face, but it was enough to show that he intended to be guarded during the rest of the conversation.

"Oh yes," he said. "I believe one of my men hired you to move the Mandan Stone to the University."

"Your man's name was Morton," replied Lou Gates, "and he didn't hire me. He hired my partner. Furthermore, he made some secret arrangements that I didn't know about."

"Secret arrangements?"

"The truck was stopped on the highway and the stone we were carrying was taken away from us and another one put in its place."

Whiz Walton cut in. "Huddlebeck," he said, "don't try to tell us you didn't know about that arrangement!"

Huddlebeck smiled thinly. "There's no use trying to fool each other," he said. He turned to Hamilton Quest. "According to the papers, that little trick caused you a good deal of embarrassment. I'm sorry about that, Mr. Quest."

"That ain't all yo' did," put in Gulliver. "Yo' sent a blubber-built critter to coyote around our house! Yo' had him rig up a fancy electric gimmick so's yo' could git down all that we said. What's more, that same slab-sided sidewinder cracked me on the head when I warn't lookin'. On top o' that—"

Hamilton Quest cut in quickly before Gulliver could mention Gleason's death. "Huddlebeck," he said, "our indictment has a number of points."

Huddlebeck's smile was disarmingly frank, but its effectiveness was lost in the face of Gleason's murder. "Try to look at it my way," he said. "I have a tremendous investment in this country. I have an organization to exploit the discovery of uranium. I can provide jobs for a lot of men and supply the government with a vital mineral."

"All of which can also be done by another mining company, or by the government itself," Hamilton Quest said, "the difference being that the Mandan Indians would profit instead of Hector Huddlebeck. You know very well, Huddlebeck, that the land on which the uranium was found belongs to the Indians. The Mandan Stone is proof of that."

"It might have been," said Huddlebeck, "but it isn't any longer."

"Why?"

"It has been destroyed."

"I don't believe it."

Whiz Walton spoke. "If you listened to the wire recording of our conversation, you know that we don't think Wahkee turned over the Mandan Stone to Gates and Gleason when they came here with the truck."

"Oh, that." Huddlebeck waved his hand airily. "Of course I know that. As soon as we learned that the stone was still in the possession of Wahkee, we came here and negotiated with the young chief."

"Huddlebeck," said Hamilton Quest, "I don't believe you."

"You don't?"

"No. Wahkee would not turn over the stone to you without first consulting me."

"But he did."

"I," said Gulliver, "hanker to know more about them there negotiations. Yo' couldn't o' made Wahkee break his promise to Mr. Quest for cash money. An' yo' couldn't do it by torture. I know somethin' about these here Mandan Injuns. They's nothin' yo' can do to them that'll make 'em holler 'uncle.' I know about some o' their religious ceremonies. They do painful things that'd make yo' flesh crawl, an' give yo' nightmares that'd make yo' leap out o' bed with the jumpin' jitters."

"The answer is quite simple," Huddlebeck replied. "I simply promised that Wahkee and his people would share equally in the profits from the uranium. Then Wahkee aided me in the destruction of the stone, so there could be no hitch in my title to the property. If you care to see for yourself, you might go to a large pile of rocks just ten feet from the roadway in the direction of my camp. There you will see where the stone was broken into bits and ground to powder."

"Where is Wahkee?" asked Hamilton Quest.

"How should I know?" Huddlebeck replied.

"Are yo'," said Gulliver, "tryin' to tell us yo' don't know where he's at?"

"I am telling you," retorted the other. "I met him a day or so ago when he was hunting. I invited him to talk the situation over. He came to my place, and we had no difficulty entering into an agreement, after which Wah-

kee aided in the destruction of the stone. Then we separated. I returned to my camp with—with several of my
men, and he came in this direction."

"So that's your story, eh?" Whiz Walton said.

"That is my story. Do you think you can prove other-
wise?" Huddlebeck turned toward Tom's father. "You
have come here on a wild-goose chase. I am sorry your
reputation had to suffer, Mr. Quest. I am an influential
man. Perhaps I can do something to repair the damage
I have done you. If so, please do not hesitate to call on
me. Now I must bid you good day."

Huddlebeck turned and walked away with long strides
and without a backward glance.

"I think he's lying," Tom Quest said emphatically.
"What do you think, Dad?"

"I am sure of one thing, Tom. I am sure that Wahkee
would not have made any such agreement before consulting me."

"If Huddlebeck lied about that," replied the boy, "he
probably lied about everything else, including the fact
that he doesn't know where Wahkee is."

"Do you think he's holding Wahkee prisoner?" asked
Whiz Walton.

"It is quite possible."

"Then why don't we go to his hangout?" demanded
Gulliver.

"I intend to, but I shall go alone."

"Alone?" echoed Tom. "Dad, that would be dangerous!"

"Think it over, Tom, and you will realize that it would be far less dangerous for me to go alone than for all of us to go together."

"Yo' couldn't put up no fight," argued Gulliver.

"That, Gulliver, is just the point. If we go there in force, there is likely to be a fight. But if I go alone, unarmed, Huddlebeck could hardly use violence, especially if he knew that the rest of you would be waiting for me to return."

"I don't like it, Dad. Besides, what can you accomplish by going there?"

"What's your plan?" asked Whiz Walton.

"I have no plan. I shall simply keep my eyes open while I am in Huddlebeck's place. If Wahkee is held a prisoner there, he will find some way to let me know."

Tom said, "Do you think it would be worth while looking over the place where Huddlebeck said the stone was broken up?"

"It would be a waste of time, son. We probably would find crushed stone which would prove nothing. No, I think my plan is better. The rest of you wait here or in the lodge with Wahkee's father. I'll be back in a little while."

CHAPTER 20

To the Aid of Mah-to

W<small>ELL</small>," observed Whiz Walton after Hamilton Quest disappeared in the woods, "it looks as if we're stuck. Does anyone want to do the town?"

"Do what?" asked Gulliver, looking at the columnist.

"Look the Mandans over. Investigate their living quarters and get acquainted with a few of them."

Lou Gates was rolling up his sleeves. "You three do what you want," he said. "I'm going to do some work on Mr. Quest's car. The spark plugs and points need cleaning, and I think the timing is off a little. While I'm at it, he continued, turning toward Gulliver, "I'll give the jeep a tune-up."

"Yo' better not," warned Gulliver. "I don't want no

one to go messin' around with the innards o' my jeep!"

Whiz Walton glanced at his wrist watch and saw that it was nearly noon. "I wonder how long Mr. Quest will be gone," he said.

Tom said, "Your guess is as good as mine, Whiz."

"I know what I'm going to do."

"What?"

The columnist pointed to the circle of Mandan houses. "I'm going to get better acquainted with the chief."

"War-rah-pa?"

"Yes. Maybe I can find a human-interest story there. Want to come along, Tom?"

"I'd rather get acquainted with the medicine man."

"Tom, yo' speakin' o' that blubberface that's with War-rah-pa?"

"No, Gulliver. I mean the little fellow who gave you the pocket mirror."

"Oh, him." Gulliver grinned and brought the gift from the pocket of his dungarees. He eyed it in the palm of his hand and chuckled throatily. "Givin' me an ad for beauty soap!" he said. "Why, that wrinkled-up old goat!"

"That mirror," said Tom, "was probably one of his most prized possessions. Maybe we should repay him."

"Yo' mean give him a present?"

"Why not?"

Gulliver seemed pleased with the idea. "I can probably

find somethin' in my medicine chest that'd tickle the old critter fit to kill. Maybe we could take him somethin' that'd be like magic—sort of."

"Good idea," agreed Tom heartily.

Gulliver reached over the side of the jeep and threw back the lid of his priceless chest. "I wish," he said, "we had some o' that junk we took to the head-hunters in Ecuador. Them fancy beads 'n tinsel trinkets would be right in the groove."

"Wait!" Tom said, reaching into the chest. "How's this?"

It was a small nickel-plated pocket flashlight, hardly larger than a man-sized fountain pen.

"Does she work?"

Tom pressed the button and the small lamp glowed.

Gulliver said, "Good enough. Now maybe we can find some other things."

Tom held the electric torch while Gulliver pawed through the contents of the chest and found a pair of very large horn-rimmed sunglasses, with one blue lens and an open space where the other lens had been.

"Take these," he said, handing the glasses to Tom. "I always figured I'd git another lens put into these some-day, but I never did git around to it. An' here's somethin' else."

It was a nautical cap that had once been white, with a black patent-leather visor.

"That," said Tom, "is the cap Captain Popple gave you."

"I never could wear it on account of it bein' about six sizes too small. Maybe it'll fit old Wishbone. His ears was about as close together as Popple's."

He slammed down the lid of his chest, saying, "I reckon we're all set."

Tom looked at Whiz Walton and said, "You're going to pay War-rah-pa a call, eh, Whiz?"

"Yeah."

"We'll join you in his lodge after we've seen Mah-to."

"Okay, Tom. See you later."

As the columnist moved away, Lou Gates straightened up from the engine of Quest's coupé, holding a spark plug. "Look at this," he said happily. "The plugs are a mess."

Gulliver eyed the truck driver, who was smeared with black grease to the elbows. "So are yo'," he observed. "Have a good time. We'll see yo' later."

Mah-to lived alone. His house, which was the smallest in the village, was apart from the circle. The little medicine man was standing in the doorway as Tom Quest and Gulliver approached. When he saw them, he ducked inside, reappearing an instant later with a hideous profusion of huge teeth hanging over his lower lip.

"Leapin' catamounts!" cried Gulliver. "What's he done with his face?"

Tom laughed. "A set of trick teeth," he said. "I've seen them in the novelty stores. They're made out of celluloid. I wonder where he got them."

Mah-to removed the teeth and gave a "come-on" gesture. Then he disappeared a second time and bobbed back, squirrel-like, holding a drum in one hand and a drumstick in the other. He thumped the drum enthusiastically until his guests were at his side.

At the doorway Gulliver sniffed the air. "Somethin'," he said, "stinks."

The odor was like perfume or toilet water, and not at all unpleasant.

Mah-to said, "You come. You call on Mah-to. That good. Inside me show great medicine."

"We brought some gifts for you," said Tom Quest. He handed Mah-to the flashlight and showed the little Indian how to work it.

Mah-to reacted like a small child. He beamed delightedly and flashed the light in all directions.

"Here's some more stuff for yo'," said Gulliver. He hung the glasses on Mah-to's face, then set the nautical cap on the medicine man's head at a rakish angle.

"Now," he said, "yo' look downright smart." He held up the pocket mirror. "Take a look at yo'self."

Mah-to squinted in the mirror with first one eye closed and then the other. He favored Tom with a toothless grin, then turning to Gulliver, he said, "You good. Mah-to like."

"All right, all right," said Gulliver, squirming uncomfortably.

"Mah-to like much." He reached out with a wrinkled hand and patted the big man's granite-like cheek.

Gulliver muttered something that sounded like "Aw-w-wk."

Then Mah-to scurried across the room and stuck his arm beneath a pile of buffalo skins. "Me give present," he said. "Me give great present!'

He brought his hand out gripping the sort of bottle one sees on the shelf in barber shops. He held it out at arm's length and sprayed it with the flashlight beam.

Tom saw that the gaudy label, in letters of gold, said, "Lilac."

"Now make good magic!" Mah-to said. He pulled the stopper from the bottle and, without warning, liberally doused Gulliver with the cloying scent.

The big man leaped back howling. "What yo' done to me!" he thundered, and then he wailed, "Oh, Tom!"

Tom laughed heartily. It was a minute before he could speak. "It won't kill you, Gulliver," he said.

"The smell!"

"It will soon evaporate. The smell won't stay with you very long."

"It'll be with me 'til we git back to Whiz Walton, an' he'll have a-plenty to say!" Gulliver swung toward Mah-to, who had upended the bottle to take a swallow of the aromatic fluid.

The Adam's apple in his skinny neck bobbed up and down a few times. Then he offered the bottle to Gulliver.

"Good medicine," he beamed.

Gulliver could only grunt despondently.

Then Mah-to became serious. With preliminary courtesies disposed of by the exchange of gifts, he seemed inclined to unburden his troubles and found Tom Quest a sympathetic listener.

He told Tom how he had been the medicine man of the Mandan village, with a great deal of power and influence, until the old chief had called a meeting in the council ring and announced that there would be a new medicine man whose every command must be obeyed.

Little Mah-to had been deeply hurt. His pride had suffered immeasurably. He had spent one entire night supplicating the Mandan gods to restore him to his high position.

Mah-to's English vocabulary was meager, and it took the better part of an hour to tell his story. Tom listened attentively, but Gulliver was sulky. He sat near the door, apart from Tom and Mah-to, and from time to time he turned his head and sniffed at the sleeve of his shirt.

"What can we do about it, Gulliver?" Tom asked suddenly.

"I dunno, Tom, unless I burn my clothes. Once these heavy woolen shirts git a-hold o' somethin', they hang on to it.

"I once tangled with a polecat an' I tried washin' my clothes in everythin'. I even rolled 'em in the barnyard but that polecat smell stayed just as lively as ever. An' this here stuff will do the same."

"I'm not talking about your shirt," laughed Tom. "We've got to find some way to fix up Mah-to's troubles."

Gulliver sniffed his sleeve and made a wry face. "He sure fixed me up," he said. Then, "What do yo' mean, Tom—'fix him up'?"

"Didn't you listen to what he was telling us? We've got to do something that will make him a greater medicine man than that fat Indian War-rah-pa brought into the village."

"That jowlface!" said Gulliver scornfully. "I didn't like his looks. He's too doggoned smug an' satisfied with himself. I'd like to do somethin' that'd make him jump. I—" The big man broke off. For the first time since arriving at Mah-to's house, the deep frown left his face.

"Have you an idea?"

"Maybe so, Tom. Let me think a minute." During a brief silence Gulliver thought hard and the working of his mind was reflected by a tense expression and a rasping of his big thumbnail on the bristly stubble of his chin.

Then he smacked a fist against a huge palm, and said, "I got it! Yo', Tom, follow me, an' bring Mah-to along! We're goin' to fix up somethin' in the jeep, then go collect old hogjowls an' show him medicine he never saw before!"

Gulliver's mood had suddenly changed to one of hearty geniality. "Cheer up, Mah-to," he said. "When I git done, yo're goin' to rule the roost agin!"

CHAPTER 21

A Shocking Surprise

WHIL WALTON found it comparatively easy to converse
with Wahkee's father, the aged War-rah-pa. The chief
had learned enough English from Hamilton Quest to express himself. He was perfectly willing to talk about the
history of the Mandan people and declared that it was
his ancestors who had given sanctuary to Swedes and
Norwegians who came to the Western Hemisphere in
the fourteenth century.

As proof of this, he showed the columnist a long list of
words which had been prepared by Hamilton Quest on
a previous visit. The words were in common use in the
Mandan tongue and had a striking similarity to words
with the same meanings in Norwegian.

War-rah-pa talked about the legends, customs, rites,
and practices of his people, but whenever the reporter
tried to discuss the disappearance of Wahkee or the iden-

tity of the fat medicine man who sat near one side of the lodge, the chief had nothing to say.

Whiz Walton pointed to the five-by-five Indian, who had not spoken. "Does he understand English?" he asked.

War-rah-pa's shrug of the shoulders was meaningless, but it was his only reply.

The several women in the lodge paid no attention to the white man and the chief, who sat on buffalo robes halfway between the fireplace and the door. The women went about their household chores. Some were grinding corn; others were pounding meat to make pemmican, while another kept careful watch on something that was cooking in a kettle on the fire.

Whiz saw Gulliver approaching from the center of the open space in front of the lodge. Tom Quest was half a pace behind, trying to match the big man's long strides, and Mah-to jogged several yards behind Tom.

"Yo', Whiz!" called Gulliver as he entered War-rah-pa's lodge. "Where at is that medicine man? Oh, there yo' are."

"What's up?" asked the newshound. "Whew!" he exclaimed as Gulliver drew near. "Why, Gulliver!" he drawled, sniffing noisily. "You smell real pretty!"

Gulliver shot Whiz a sour look but did not break his stride across the flagstone floor to the man who had usurped Mah-to's place.

"We got somethin' to show yo'," he said.

The fat Indian looked up but gave no sign that he understood.

Gulliver stuck out his right hand and waggled the thick index finger. "Come on," he said.

The Indian shook his head.

"What's going on?" demanded Whiz Walton. "What do you want with him?"

"Bein' as he's a medicine man, he'll be downright interested in what we got to show him."

"Where?"

"Over at my jeep."

War-rah-pa looked uncomfortable, but said nothing.

"I reckon his nibs needs help." Gulliver squatted in front of the medicine man and grasped the leather tunic beneath the armpits. He stood, lifting the other to his feet.

"Now," he said, "yo' comin', or have I got to tote yo'?"

"He doesn't understand English," said Whiz Walton.

"He sure must savvy that I want him to come with me."

Tom Quest stepped forward. "Just a minute. Let me speak to him. I know a few words of Mandan." The boy spoke slowly, pronouncing the unfamiliar words with careful precision.

The only reply was a negative shake of the medicine man's head.

"Does that," asked Gulliver, "mean he won't come along or he don't savvy what yo' said?"

"I don't know, Gulliver."

"Well, they's nothin' to do but drag him." Gulliver grabbed the front of the tunic and literally dragged the fat medicine man from the lodge. The Indian threw up his hands to clutch the elaborate headdress of buffalo fur, porcupine quills, and eagle feathers. He held it in place but made no sound, not even one of protest.

"You better come along, Whiz," Tom Quest said as Gulliver left the lodge.

The lean columnist was on his feet. "I intend to," he said. "I'm going to see what this is all about."

Tom said, "Mah-to has been the medicine man in this village for a long time. This newcomer has no business taking his place—unless his magic is better than Mah-to's."

Whiz Walton saw a twinkle in Tom Quest's eyes. "What are you up to?" he asked in a low voice.

"Come on and see. Gulliver has tricked up the jeep."

Gulliver didn't hesitate until he had dragged the medicine man to the side of his small car. He waited until Mah-to, Whiz Walton, and Tom Quest had joined him, then signaled to Lou Gates, who had left his work on Hamilton Quest's car to aid in the "big medicine."

The hood of the jeep was raised, revealing two eight-foot lengths of wire that ran from the engine. The insulation for about a foot at the end of each wire had been scraped away.

Gulliver held one wire and Lou Gates the other. At the big man's signal Lou Gates wrapped the length of exposed copper around one of the fat Indian's wrists while Gulliver did the same on the other side.

"I showed yo' what to do, Mah-to," he said. "Git into that there seat, an' give this critter a sample o' yo' magic."

Mah-to looked at the dashboard.

"I'll help you," Tom Quest said. Stepping forward, he turned the ignition key.

"Now come foot," Mah-to said.

"That's right, Mah-to." Tom pointed to the starter button. "Just put your foot on that and when Gulliver gives the word, press down." He gestured with his hand.

The fat medicine man was trembling visibly. Several times he opened his mouth as if to speak, then closed it without speaking.

Gulliver said, "Now Mah-to, yo' tell him yo're a better medicine man than he is. Yo're goin' to prove it, then give him a chance to show some o' his magic. My bet is that he's about to lose face with everyone in this here village. Go on, Mah-to. Sound off."

Mah-to spoke. His rapid flow of Indian words was directed at his rival, who stood beside the jeep with a wire attached to each wrist. When he finished, Mah-to looked at Gulliver.

"Now stand on it."

Mah-to stepped on the starter. There was a whirrr and the unmuffled engine roared, but above the popping explosions shrill cries of fear and anguish filled the air.

The medicine man leaped wildly, throwing his arms in great circles and shrieking as if a thousand imps were torturing him with red-hot needles, as the high-frequency current from the spark plugs shot into his wrists.

During his wild gyrations the buffalo-skin headdress slid to the ground. It was Gulliver who yelled then.

"Cut that motor!"

Tom Quest leaped to cut the switch.

Whiz Walton stared incredulously and so did Mah-to.

Beneath the headdress, the fat man's head was bald. The skin was pink and there was a definite line of demarcation where the dark part of the forehead ended.

"He's not an Indian at all!" cried Whiz Walton.

"Yo're tellin' me!" exploded Gulliver. "Did yo' hear the things he was yowlin' when that electric juice went through him! He was cussin' wild an' it warn't no Injun cussin'!"

The fat man was jerking the wires from his wrists. His eyes were bloodshot with fury. Gulliver stepped forward and shot out one hand which gripped the tunic at the throat. He ripped it down the front, then crumpled it into a ball. Holding this in one hand and the back of the fat man's neck in the other, he scrubbed at the painted face. The brilliant reds and blues of war paint were rubbed off and with it came some of the brown stain.

"No Injun at all!" growled Gulliver while he worked.

"I know him!" cut in Tom Quest quickly. "It's the fat man, Gulliver! It's the man who had the wire recorder in the barn!"

"Yo' mean the one that cracked me on the head—the one that locked us in that room?"

"Yes!" replied the boy excitedly. "The same one!"

"Great day in the mornin'!"

The fat man's rage gave way to fear. He seemed to wilt in Gulliver's strong grip. One hand crept toward the buttons of the shirt he had worn beneath the tunic.

"None o' that!" roared Gulliver, slapping the fat hand aside.

He ripped open the shirt and reached beneath it.

"Packin' a gun, eh?" he said as he brought out a heavy weapon that had been tucked in a band around the fat man's waist.

"Well, now we got some things to talk about!"

CHAPTER 22

To Arms!

GULLIVER hefted the big gun that he had taken from the fat man. He thumbed back the catch and flipped the cylinder sideways, then dumped the cartridges into the palm of his huge hand and put them into his pocket. He closed the cylinder and, gripping the handle of the gun, slapped the long barrel against his leg. Then he looked wistfully at the shiny bald head of the fat man, who was now seated cross-legged on the flagstone floor of War-rah-pa's lodge, his hands tied together at the wrists.

Whiz Walton looked at Gulliver and said, "A penny for your thoughts."

"That blubberface whammed the top o' my head with this here gun when me an' Tom was lookin' at the wire recorder. I was just thinkin' what a crease I could make in the top o' that shiny head by doin' the same to him."

War-rah-pa was the only one who was not surprised by

the discovery that the fat man was no Indian. The old chief had been visibly shaken when Gulliver and Lou Gates had marched the prisoner into the lodge with Tom and Whiz Walton following.

"You can't hit him now, Gulliver," Tom Quest said. "His hands are tied, and besides—"

"Don't worry, Tom. I don't aim to mess him up. We'll just hold him here 'til yo' dad gits back."

War-rah-pa shook his head slowly. Tom Quest was the only one who saw the gesture.

"What's the matter, War-rah-pa?" he asked.

"Me not like," replied the Indian.

"Yo' don't like what?" demanded Gulliver.

War-rah-pa looked uncertain. Before he could reply, the fat man spoke. "You're going to like it even less if you don't do something about these white men." The fat man's small eyes were still bloodshot with anger. "You'd better untie my hands and let me go right away or—well, you know what'll happen."

Gulliver stepped forward. "Just what," he rumbled, "will happen?"

"The old chief knows. If he expects to see his son alive he'd better act fast." Turning to the chief, the fat man continued, "You're the leader of this village. Call in your people. Tell them to make prisoners of these four and turn me loose!"

"If he tries anythin' like that," threatened Gulliver, "there'll be a fight that'll make these Injuns think an earthquake has busted loose on the back of a buckin' bronco."

"If he doesn't, he'll never see his son alive!"

"Yo' speakin' o' Wahkee?"

The fat man replied, "Yes."

"Hold on!" cut in Whiz Walton sharply. "I begin to see the pattern!" He turned to War-rah-pa. "When this man came here, he told you that your son had been captured by the white men who want the stone. He told you he would stay here as medicine man and give you orders that would have to be obeyed to protect the life of Wahkee. Isn't that right?"

War-rah-pa nodded.

"In that case," put in Tom Quest, "Huddlebeck lied to us when he said that Wahkee wasn't being held prisoner!"

"Of course he lied to us," replied the columnist, "and your father knew it. He knew that Wahkee wouldn't make a deal."

The fat man said, "What about it, War-rah-pa? Are you going to set me free?"

The chief's dark eyes were fixed for a moment on the fat man, then they moved slowly to Gulliver. "You," he said slowly, "good medicine."

"Yo' mean yo're goin' to let me handle this here situation?" demanded Gulliver in a somewhat belligerent voice.

"You boss."

"Now we got that settled," Gulliver replied, "one of us is goin' to stay here all the time to keep an eye on the prisoner." He reloaded the gun he had taken from the fat man and passed it to Tom Quest. "Yo', Tom, stay here an' stand guard."

"Where are you going, Gulliver?"

"I'm goin' to unhook those wires from my jeep an' close the hood." Gulliver turned to Whiz and Gates.

"Yo' want to come along?"

"Might as well," replied Whiz Walton, sensing that Gulliver had something to discuss.

At the door, Gulliver turned back and said, "Tom, if they's any sign o' trouble, just fire that gun an' we'll come on the run."

"All right, Gulliver."

The big man started talking as he strode across the council ring between Whiz Walton and Lou Gates. "No one has made mention o' the fact," he said, "but they's been a-plenty o' time for Quest to git back from that meetin' with Huddlebeck."

"I've been thinking the same thing," replied the newshound.

"And so has Tom Quest. I've seen him lookin' at his watch downright frequent. He ain't said nothin', but I know he's worried."

"There's reason to be worried."

"Why do yo' say that, Whiz?"

"Can't you guess?"

"Yeah, but tell me what yo' think."

"Well," the columnist said, "Huddlebeck will stop at nothing to get possession of the Mandan Stone. Wahkee is the only one who knows where it's hidden. Wahkee couldn't be made to talk by any amount of torture. He'd die before he'd break his word to Mr. Quest. Huddlebeck has had ample opportunity to find that out. On the other hand, Wahkee probably would be quick to talk if the life of Hamilton Quest were in danger."

"That," said Gulliver, "is just what I been thinkin'."

Lou Gates said, "Do you think Quest has been captured by those crooks?"

"I think," said Gulliver, "the three of us should go to that there Huddlebeck place an' find out."

"What about Tom Quest?" asked Whiz.

Gulliver said, "We'll have to go there geared for trouble, which same we'll likely find. Huddlebeck has got at least half a dozen men. If things are like we figure, there'll be gunplay an' people will git hurt."

They had reached the jeep. Gulliver jerked loose the

wires that were connected to the spark plugs, then lowered and clamped the hood.

"I got extra guns in here," he said, throwing open the lid of his medicine chest and reaching inside.

"I'd hate to have Tom think we ran out on him."

"We won't run out, Whiz. I wanted to sound out yo' two an' see if yo' was willin' to go with me to Huddlebeck's place, before I spoke to Tom."

"You can count on me," Lou Gates said.

"And me," added Whiz Walton. "You know that."

Gulliver passed out weapons with holsters and cartridge belts. "I'll tell Tom what we aim to do," he said. "Likewise, I'll tell him someone has to stay here to make sure the fat man don't talk War-rah-pa into settin' him free. I'll convince him that he's the one to stay, an' then the rest of us will go an' git Hamilton Quest an' Wahkee."

Wahkee was dead.

This fact alone saved Hamilton Quest untold tortures. Hector Huddlebeck would have acted exactly as Whiz Walton surmised, had the youthful Mandan chief still been alive. He would have tortured Quest until Wahkee revealed the hiding place of the Mandan Stone, but with Wahkee dead, there was nothing to be gained by threats of torture.

Huddlebeck had other plans which he began to put into effect as soon as Tom Quest's father arrived at the rambling log building in the woods.

Quest knew that he had made a serious mistake in going there, as soon as he stepped through the door. He knew it by the ruthless expression in Hector Huddlebeck's face. He knew it by the hard edge in Huddlebeck's voice when he said without the slightest trace of cordiality, "I'm glad you're here, Quest."

Huddlebeck turned to four men with sullen faces, standing in the big living room, and said, "Tie him and gag him."

Two of the men stepped forward without a word, seized the explorer roughly, and twisted his hands behind his back.

"You see," said Huddlebeck, "I thought you'd come here and I was ready for you."

"What are you going to do?" demanded Quest.

"I am going to hold you until your friends come looking for you. Then we'll hold them until—"

After a pause Quest said, "Until when?"

"You," replied Hector Huddlebeck, "will find out soon enough!"

CHAPTER 23

The Torture
Chamber

WHILE TWO of the hard-faced men tied Hamilton ,
Quest's hands, a third stood guard with an ugly, short-
barreled gun of high caliber that he had drawn with
practiced skill from a shoulder holster beneath his dou-
ble-breasted coat. The fourth ruffian moved about the
room with a cigarette lighter, lighting the many oil lamps
to dispell the gathering darkness.

Hector Huddlebeck sat on a large davenport, leaning
back with his knees crossed.

Hamilton Quest took in the details of the room. It was
a huge room nearly forty feet in length with a ceiling
twice as high as the average. It occupied the entire front
portion of the rambling building. At one end an archway

opened into a corridor that seemed to run back through a large wing at right angles to the main part of the house. There were huge stone fireplaces at both ends of the room, and above these hung mounted buffalo heads. The mounted horns and stuffed heads of other animals were arranged on the walls, and the other decorations consisted of Indian weapons and shields, and a few well-chosen pictures.

There were shelves of books, and cases that held rifles and shotguns behind glass doors. Buffalo skins were spread on the plank floor. The furniture was comfortable looking and well arranged. It might have been the dream house of a wealthy sportsman. Everything about the room was of good quality, but the charm of the place was utterly destroyed by the type of men who occupied it.

Except for Huddlebeck himself, they were swarthy-skinned individuals whose faces were indelibly stamped by lives of ruthless evil. They were of the type known during a certain era as public enemies or gangsters. Their eyes were furtive and suspicious and their mouths cruel and self-indulgent.

When Hamilton Quest had been tied and gagged, Huddlebeck said, "Take him to the back room, Joe. We'll hold him there."

The man called Joe said, "You mean in the same room with the Indian?"

"Yes."

"But the Indian is dead."

Huddlebeck looked coldly at Joe without comment.

"Okay," Joe said, shrugging his shoulders. "I don't suppose it matters none."

As Hamilton Quest was led away, he heard another order in Hector Huddlebeck's clipped voice. "It's getting dark, and I don't want to be taken by surprise. You'd better turn loose the dogs."

At one side of the long corridor a door stood open. Hamilton Quest caught a passing view of a large dining room and through another door a kitchen. He passed many other doors on both sides of the corridor and judged that these gave access to bedrooms and work-rooms. There was one door at the far end of the hall. Quest halted.

"It's unlocked," the man behind him said, jabbing his back with the gun. "Push it open with your foot."

Hamilton Quest obeyed. The door swung inward quietly to reveal a small room about twelve feet square.

Twilight was rapidly deepening to darkness outside the house and the light that came through a single window was barely enough to reveal the meager furnishings. There were wooden benches along one wall, a crude table in the center, and two bunks against the wall opposite the benches. One of the bunks was occupied.

"That," said Joe, noting that Hamilton Quest's eyes were on the still form on the bunk, "is what's left of Wahkee. He won't bother you none. He died last night while we were working on him to make him tell where he'd hid that hunk of stone the boss wants."

Heavy footsteps sounded in the corridor. "Light the lamp," directed Huddlebeck as he entered the room.

Joe holstered his gun to obey.

"Huddlebeck, you'll pay for this!" Hamilton Quest said slowly, in a cold voice that revealed none of the sorrow he felt at the tragic fate of his good friend.

"Sit down on that bunk!" Huddlebeck accompanied the order with a shove that caught the elderly explorer off balance. He stumbled and fell sideways to the empty bunk.

Yellow light flickered uncertainly, then steadied and grew brighter as Joe set the glass chimney in place on the burner of the oil lamp which hung suspended from the ceiling, above the table.

The illumination revealed grim evidence that made Quest's heart beat faster. Wahkee's lifeless face was cruelly battered. His naked torso was marked and there were stains on the bunk and on the floor that gave mute testimony to the tortures the young chief had endured before death brought a merciful release.

Throaty barking of big dogs came from somewhere outside.

"My dogs," said Huddlebeck by way of explanation, "are the biggest and most vicious dogs you've ever seen. They are well trained to sound an alarm when anyone approaches this house. Those dogs are killers. They're barking now because they're glad to be released from the kennel. They'll quiet down in a few minutes. Then they'll make no more noise until your friends come here to find out why you haven't returned to the Mandan village!"

24

Trapped by the Enemy

GULLIVER SQUIRMED and fidgeted as he stood with Tom Quest in War-rah-pa's lodge. He kicked at a small insect crawling along a flagstone, looked up at Tom, then quickly dropped his eyes before the boy's steady gaze.

"Yo' see, Tom, we—uh—that is, me an' Whiz an' Gates—uh—the three of us, we sort o' talked it all over an'—uh—" He stuck his hand down the open neck of his shirt and tried to scratch an inaccessible spot on his back.

"The truth is," broke in Tom Quest, "you three want to go and see what's happened to Dad, and you don't want me to go with you. Isn't that it?"

"Well, now—uh—Tom, that ain't the way to put it."

The big man was very ill at ease. He scratched the back of his neck, then looked up as Tom said, "Why not?"

"Huh? Why not what?"

"Why can't I go with you?"

"Someone has to stay here to keep an eye on that fat skunk." Gulliver nodded toward the prisoner, who still sat on the floor with his hands tied.

"I examined his ropes while you and the others were out of the lodge. He can't get free."

"Not by himself, Tom, but War-rah-pa will be here in the lodge with him, an' so will the squaws. He might persuade one o' them to set him loose."

"There are at least six or seven men in that Huddle-beck outfit."

"Humph!" snorted Gulliver deprecatingly. "Six or seven! What's that compared to me an' Gates? The two of us could likely handle 'em even without Whiz Walton."

"You don't think I'd be any help if it came to a fight?"

"Dad-rat it, Tom!" exploded Gulliver. "I ain't no hand at whiffle-whoofin' around the bush!"

"Then get to the point, Gulliver."

"The point's just this. We figure somethin' has happened to keep yo' dad from gittin' back. The three of us are goin' to find out what it is. If them Huddlebeck dogfaces want to make somethin' of it, we'll be geared for trouble. There may be shootin' an' there may be some men killed. Yo' dad would hold it ag'in me if I let yo' into anythin' o' that sort. Besides, we do need someone here to keep an eye on jellybelly, an' yo're elected."

"Elected my eye!" retorted Tom. "I didn't have a vote!"

"Yo' don't git none. I'm votin' for yo'. Now are yo' goin' to stay here, or have I got to hogtie yo', too?"

"Try it!" retorted Tom hotly.

Gulliver compressed his lips and sucked a deep breath through his nostrils. He exhaled explosively, saying, "By gobs!"

Tom's face relaxed in a slight smile. "All right, Gulliver," he said, "you win. But get Dad back here as soon as you can."

"I aim to," promised Gulliver.

"It's nearly dark. Will you be able to find Huddle-beck's place?"

"Mah-to told us how to git there. It ain't hard to find, if a man's got sense enough to follow his nose." The big man crossed to the side of the prisoner and, in the light that came from the fire pit in the center of the room, in-spected the cords that tied his hands.

"Are you afraid I'll get loose?" the fat man sneered.

"Not by a darn sight. I aim to make dead sure yo' don't

git loose!" Gulliver pulled up the tail of the light shirt that the fat man had worn beneath the ripped-off doeskin tunic. He split the shirt up the back, then jerked it off in two pieces, exposing a naked torso that was an unhealthy pasty white in color.

With a few deft movements Gulliver tore the shirt into strips about three inches wide. He knotted these together, then wrapped them around the fat man's ankles. When he finished he stood up and surveyed his work.

"That," he said with a grunt of satisfaction, "had oughta hold yo'."

Fat lay in rolls above the prisoner's belt. His upper arms were equally flabby and almost as large as Gulliver's. The difference lay in the fact that Gulliver's biceps were muscle-sheathed and hard as rock, whereas the fat man's arms were soft and shook like jelly when Gulliver delivered a light slap for the sole purpose of adding to the prisoner's rage.

"Before I'm done with yo'," he said, "I aim to square things for the crack yo' gave me on the head, but that can keep 'til later. It's a case o' business before pleasure."

Whiz Walton called from outside the lodge. "We're waiting for you, Gulliver!"

"Be with yo' in a second, Whiz!" bellowed the big man. "I'm just tuckin' Fatty in for the night." Reaching, he hooked the fingers of his right hand beneath the front of the fat man's belt, and dragged the prisoner across the flagstone floor to the darkest, most remote part of the lodge.

By way of explanation, Gulliver said, "I'll git yo' out o' the way so's the rest o' the people in this here lodge won't have to look at yo'."

"Hey, Gulliver!" called Whiz again. "It's almost dark. Let's get going."

"Comin'!" replied Gulliver. To Tom, he said, "Yo' ain't sore?"

Tom Quest shook his head. "I'd like to go with you, Gulliver," he said, "but I—well, I guess maybe you're the one to give orders."

Gulliver shook hands, then slapped his young friend on the back and said, "Don't worry, son, we'll soon be back with yo' dad."

Looking past Tom Quest, he added, "What's more, War-rah-pa, we'll bring back yo' son Wahkee."

War-rah-pa, sitting silently, did not look up. His dark eyes were fixed in a steady gaze on the flames that leaped from the pit in the center of the lodge.

The trail through the woods was easy to follow despite the darkness. Scrubby brush and second-growth timber had been cut away to make a wide path over which building materials and furniture for Huddlebeck's house had been transported.

Gulliver led the way with an electric torch which he flashed on the hard ground intermittently. Whiz Walton walked close behind the big man and Lou Gates brought up the rear.

Presently a number of lighted windows showed up as luminous squares against the black background of forest. Gulliver halted and turned to the others.

"From here on," he whispered huskily, "we got to go real quiet. When we git close to the house we'll walk around it an' see if we can learn anything by peekin' through the windows. If that don't git us anywhere, we'll rap on the door. When it's opened, we'll rush in fast with our guns drawn. From there on, yo' two back my play, whatever it is."

Whiz Walton and Gates voiced soft agreement.

Despite his bulk, Gulliver could move as softly as a shadow. It was a trick of shifting the weight slowly from one foot to the other that he had learned in many years of stalking game in jungle country. Near the house he tucked his flashlight in a hip pocket and loosened the gun in its holster so he could draw it quickly if necessary.

He was within fifty feet of the house and his companions were right behind him, when the dogs began to bark. After sounding a warning, the two Great Danes charged the intruders.

One came at Gulliver out of the darkness in a mighty leap. The attack was so sudden and unexpected that Gulliver was caught off balance. He stumbled backward against Whiz Walton, and the two fell to the ground.

The other dog had leaped at Gates. Its mighty jaws gripped his right arm just above the wrist. Gates cried out in alarm and tried to reach his gun, but the movement only caused the dog to clamp down harder.

"Get off me!" cried Whiz Walton from somewhere beneath Gulliver's heavy torso.

Gulliver was trying to regain his feet, but each move seemed to increase the fury of the snarling animal.

The door of the house flew open and four men came out on the run. Huddlebeck shouted a command to the dogs from the doorway. At the sound of his voice, the animals drew back and subsided.

Light from electric lanterns flooded the scene, and a voice from behind one of the lights said, "You're covered. Get to your feet and keep your hands where we can see them."

Gulliver leaped to his feet with a defiant cry. His right hand dropped to his gun butt. There was a sharp crack and a stab of flame.

Gulliver jerked his hand instinctively as a bullet seared his knuckles.

"Any more of that," snapped a voice, "and I'll shoot your arm off!"

"Watch it, Gulliver!" cried Whiz Walton. "We're covered!"

"Disarm them and bring them in here!" called Huddlebeck from the doorway.

The man called Joe collected weapons from the trio, then pointed to the house and said, "Get goin'. We been expectin' you."

CHAPTER 25

Promise of Death

GULLIVER WALKED toward the door of Huddlebeck's house as slowly as possible, while he tried to estimate the strength and distribution of the enemy. Flashlights carried by men who walked behind Whiz Walton and Lou Gates marked two of Huddlebeck's men. There were at least two others in the darkness. Beyond doubt all four had guns. Also in the darkness, Gulliver could hear the throaty growls of the Great Danes. He decided to postpone a quick explosion into violence until he was inside the lighted house. But the big man never had a chance.

As he stepped through the doorway, a blackjack in the hand of a swarthy half-breed crashed against the back of his head. Gulliver's knees buckled. He slumped to the floor and fell face forward.

Two men were on him instantly. They grabbed his

arms and fastened them together behind his back with many turns of wire.

Meanwhile, Whiz Walton and Lou Gates were seized by others. Their hands were tied behind their backs, but they had escaped a knockout by a blackjack.

Gulliver was stunned for only a few minutes, but it was long enough for Huddlebeck's men to render the big fellow helpless. He regained consciousness as the half-breed spoke.

"You say, Señor Huddlebeck, that we are to take no chances weet the beeg one."

"He'll not make any trouble for us now, Miguel," Huddlebeck replied.

The dark-skinned man called Joe said, "He's comin' around."

Gulliver opened his eyes and realized instantly that his opportunity for a sudden attack with fists was gone. He looked at Whiz Walton, then at Huddlebeck.

"I suppose," said Huddlebeck, "you came here looking for your friend."

"What," demanded Gulliver, "have yo' done with him?"

"You'll join him presently. He's in the back room."

"See here, Huddlebeck," Whiz Walton said, "you're carrying on in a pretty high-handed way. Do you really think you can get away with this?"

"If I didn't expect to get away with it, I wouldn't have tried it," returned the mining operator. "You're probably wondering about your future. Well, I can assure you, you won't have one much longer."

A pasty-faced man of medium size came from another part of the building and spoke to Huddlebeck in an ingratiating voice. "Everything is fixed in the rear room, sir."

"You've spread old rags and shavings on the floor?"

"No sir, I didn't spread them around. I left them in a pile in one corner. If you want them spread around, Mr. Huddlebeck, I—"

"It doesn't matter, Morton. Perhaps they'll start a more effective fire if they're heaped up in one corner. Did you saturate the stuff with oil?"

"Yes, sir. We can start the fire when you give the word."

"Fire!" exclaimed Whiz Walton.

"What do yo' aim to do?" Gulliver demanded.

"Unfortunately," Huddlebeck replied, "just one man knew where the Mandan Stone was hidden. He died last night."

"You mean to say you murdered Wahkee?" Lou Gates gasped.

"He died last night," repeated Huddlebeck. "And so, we cannot locate the Mandan Stone. It is too bad Mr.

Quest had to come here and interfere in my business. He has learned too much about me, so—"

"So he dies!" finished Miguel. "And all of you—you die weet heem!" The half-breed exposed his dirty yellow teeth in a leer, as if the thoughts of murder pleased his sadistic nature.

"You—"

Whiz Walton was cut off by Huddlebeck. "Please don't tell me again that I can't get away with it. There's going to be a fire in the wing of my building. Who is there to prove that your deaths were anything but a regrettable accident?"

"Lock them up!" The last was directed at the hoodlums who were in the room awaiting orders.

"How soon, señor," Miguel said, "do we 'ave the fire?"

"Not until we've got them all. There's one more in Quest's party. His son."

"Not Tom!" cried Gulliver. "They ain't no need to kill the boy!"

"Take them away."

CHAPTER 26

Tom Goes Alone

TIME DRAGGED intolerably for Tom Quest in old War-rah-pa's lodge. He sat with his back toward the fire watching the captured fat man, who lay near the wall. At fifteen-minute intervals he got up to stretch his legs and examine the ropes that held the prisoner's hands and the strips of cloth that bound his feet.

The women laid out food which neither War-rah-pa nor Tom Quest felt like eating.

After two hours had passed, the boy began to worry. There had been ample time for Gulliver and the others to reach the Huddlebeck establishment and return.

After another quarter-hour had passed, Tom Quest stepped to the door of the lodge and looked across the moonlit council ring toward the woods. He turned and was about to resume his position by the fire when Mah-to came around the side of the round-roofed building.

"Big Medicine not come back?" queried the little medicine man.

"Not yet, Mah-to."

"Him gone long time."

"Too long," replied Tom. "They should be back by now."

Mah-to stabbed Tom's chest with a clawlike finger, then touched his own flat frame. "You—me," he said, "go find."

"I'd like to go, Mah-to, but I promised Gulliver I'd stay here and keep an eye on the prisoner."

Tom saw that the figure of speech confused the little Indian. "I mean," he said, "I must stay on guard. Prisoner must not escape."

"Mah-to fix." The Indian scurried across the open area to the wooden cylinder that resembled a hogshead and held the strongest of the tribal medicine and charms.

The moon was bright enough to reveal Mah-to leaping agilely over the high side of the hogshead. A moment later he climbed out and hurried back to Tom. In one hand he clutched a bottle which he patted while he favored the boy with a toothless grin.

"Strong medicine," he said. "Make prisoner deep sleep."

"You mean it's poison?"

Mah-to shook his head. "Not dead sleep. Only deep sleep."

Before Tom could reply, the Indian was gone. Mah-to scooted across the lodge floor toward the place where the fat man lay awake and sullen.

As Tom turned to follow, War-rah-pa stood to block the way. "Mah-to," the chief said, "make good medicine. Make prisoner sleep until daylight come."

"But War-rah-pa—" objected Tom, "we can't let Mah-to—"

A scream from the far side of the lodge cut off Tom's speech and then a throaty, gargling sound, followed by an angry stream of cursing during which Mah-to rejoined Tom and War-rah-pa at the doorway.

"What did you do, Mah-to?"

The medicine man held up the bottle and inverted it to show that it was empty. He tossed it to one side, then pointed to the fat man, whose voice already had grown weaker.

"You made him drink it?"

Mah-to nodded.

"But how could you do that if he didn't want to?"

By gestures Mah-to showed how he had placed the thumb and index finger of one hand on the sides of the fat man's mouth and pressed to force the lips apart. Then he had rammed the neck of the bottle into the prisoner's mouth while with the other he held his nostrils closed. It was a simple choice of swallow the stuff or suffocate, and the fat man had swallowed. A few minutes later he was sleeping as quietly and peacefully as a chubby, over-fed baby.

Tom remained on duty for another thirty minutes, during which War-rah-pa assured the boy that Mah-to's medicine was a harmless sleeping potion. Tom looked at the luminous dial of his wrist watch. It was five minutes to eleven.

"I'll wait just five more minutes," he said. "And if Dad and Gulliver and the others aren't back by then, I'm going to go look for them."

At eleven o'clock Tom set out for the Huddlebeck building in the woods. Mah-to accompanied him to the wide path through the trees.

"From here," Tom said, "I'm going alone."

Mah-to was not pleased with this decision, but Tom remained firm because he felt that the impulsive little Indian might do something that would provoke gunplay if, and when, he learned that Wahkee had been made to suffer torture or worse.

After Mah-to had left him, Tom's eyes rapidly adjusted themselves to the darkness of the woods. Enough moon-light filtered through the leafy ceiling overhead to show the path as he walked along slowly.

Presently he saw the lighted windows of the house. He advanced as silently as Gulliver had done, pausing once to listen. He was fifty feet from the house when two big animals appeared as blobs of black on the trail ahead. Both of them barked and charged to meet the boy.

"Dogs!" thought Tom, and his heart sank. Here was a contingency none of them had anticipated.

He braced himself to meet the attack of the two Great Danes charging down the path, when suddenly a well-aimed boulder hit the ground with a vicious thud directly in front of the oncoming dogs. At the same moment, Mah-to's high-pitched cackle sounded from the deep woods beyond the edge of the trail. Instantly the two dogs halted, stiff-legged, then swerved off the trail and, with angry snarls, crashed into the underbrush in pursuit of the new intruder, whose taunting cackle sounded fainter now.

"That little monkey!" Tom thought, taking shelter among the trees that lined the trail. "He never went back at all. He was in the woods and deliberately drew the dogs away from me. Gosh, I hope Mah-to knows what he's doing."

Tom need not have worried. The wily little medicine man knew countless age-old Indian methods for shaking off pursuers, both human and canine.

Inside the house Hector Huddlebeck and several of his

men had been listening intently since the first bark.

"I'll take a look," one man said after a lengthy pause. He opened the door and pressed the button on a flashlight.

The beam pierced the darkness and swung from side to side. It flashed across the tree trunks and the underbrush in which Tom crouched.

Tom heard the man with the flashlight speak to someone in the room. "I don't see anyone."

Another voice said, "Go after them."

The man with the flashlight closed the door behind him and, crossing the trail, plunged into the woods in the direction of the now distant barking.

Tom waited in his hiding place for several minutes before venturing forward.

CHAPTER 27

Attack

Tom Quest crept to one of the lighted windows and looked into the huge, attractive living room. Hector Huddlebeck sat in an easy chair, gazing thoughtfully into the fireplace. Morton, whose name Tom did not know at the time, was at a desk making entries in some kind of ledger. A dark-skinned man with greasy-looking hair and a black mustache sat on the edge of a davenport, shaving paper-thin slices from a stick of firewood with a wicked-looking knife. Four men played cards at a table near one corner of the room.

Tom noticed that there was a significant bulge beneath their buttoned coats. "Shoulder holsters and guns," he told himself.

Rounding the corner of the house, he saw a row of windows all the same height from the ground. Huddle-

beck apparently had considered window shades unneces-
sary in the remote woods.

The first, second, and third windows in the long row
gave Tom a view of a darkened dining room. There was
a light in the next room, which proved to be a kitchen.
A big man in a lumberjack shirt sat in a tilted-back chair
with his slippered feet resting on a short ladder. By the
light of a hanging oil lamp he was reading a comic magazine and following each word with his fat index finger
while he moved his lips to form the syllables.

The next three rooms were dark, but moonlight slant-
ing past Tom's shoulder was sufficient to show that these
were bedrooms simply furnished and equipped with
double-decker bunks.

Tom moved along the "L" toward two lighted windows at the rear. He paused beneath the first of these and
ducked low. Then he raised his head slowly until he
could peer over the edge of the lighted window. He saw
two men seated on wooden chairs on opposite sides of a
hall. The men faced each other, and between the two
there was a closed door that obviously opened into the
room that had the last window in the row.

Tom moved to this and gasped at what he saw. Gulliver lay face down on the floor. His hands were wound
with wire and there was blood where the wire had cut the
flesh in the big man's efforts to get free.

Whiz Walton and Lou Gates sat on a bench. They looked strained and uncomfortable with their arms drawn behind their backs and gags distorting their faces.

Tom's father sat on the edge of a bunk. He, too, was tied and gagged, and on another bunk a blanket covered something that looked like a human form.

One corner of the room was filled with piled-up shavings, rags, and balled-up papers.

Tom pressed his face close to the window where it would be lighted by the oil lamp, then moved his hand close to the glass until he caught Whiz Walton's eye.

Whiz nudged Lou Gates, then prodded Gulliver with one toe. Gulliver rolled to his side and looked up. He, too, was gagged. Hamilton Quest followed the direction of Whiz Walton's gaze and saw his son. Tom saw new hope coming into the older man's eyes.

After a few minutes' work with the strong blade of his clasp knife pushed between the sashes, Tom managed to move the window lock aside. The window lifted easily and soundlessly. The boy climbed over the sill to the bunk beside his father and held one finger to his lips in a gesture of warning as he pointed to the door.

The keen edge of his knife soon freed his father from the gag and ropes. In a few moments' time the others were released.

Gulliver stood up and rubbed his tortured wrists and

worked his tongue and mouth. Tom whispered in the big man's ear.

"Two fellows are sitting right outside the door. There's another in the kitchen. Huddlebeck and five more men are in the living room. One man went out after the dogs."

Gulliver nodded.

"Ten altogether," whispered Whiz, "and all of them armed."

Gulliver said, "Tom, give Whiz yo' gun."

"What about you?" replied Tom in a whisper.

"Yo' said there was two men outside the door. They likely got guns. They'll do 'til I can find some better ones."

Gulliver tiptoed to the corner and selected a piece of the oil-soaked paper. "Yo' watch," he said. "I'll show yo' somethin'."

He elevated the chimney of the oil lamp and held the paper to the wick until it caught fire. Then he dropped it on the floor against the door and fanned it with his big hand.

A muffled voice came through the door saying, "Hey, Joe! I smell smoke!"

"Me, too!" said a second voice.

"Hey, look, it's comin' from inside! We'd better have a look. The boss would be sore if this place caught fire before the kid got here."

A key turned in the lock and the door swung in. Two faces with mongrel features peered inside.

Then Gulliver acted with speed and agility that were surprising in one of his size. Stamping out the burning scrap of paper, he leaped forward, grabbed one of the heads in each hand, and brought them together with a sickening thud. Both pairs of eyes glazed and the guards went limp.

"That," said Gulliver softly, "takes care o' two. We got eight to go."

Tom said, "I'll get some of the wire they used on you and tie them up."

"No need for that," replied Gulliver, reaching beneath the coats to collect the guns of the unconscious men. "Git that wire an' bring 'er along, but don't waste time on these two. They'll be out for as long as this'll take."

He gave one gun to Hamilton Quest, the other to Lou Gates. To Tom he said, "Stay back. I'll go ahead."

"But Gulliver," argued Tom, "you're not armed."

"Who ain't armed?" retorted Gulliver, holding up two balled fists. "I'm packin' batterin' rams!"

With catlike steps he moved down the corridor to the kitchen door and jerked it open. The cook looked up and his mouth went wide, but he had no chance to speak.

Gulliver's open hand, with fingers stiff, came in from the side like a meat cleaver to a sensitive spot on the cook's neck. The comic magazine dropped from limp fingers to the floor and the big cook fell on top of it.

But that was the end of stealth. In falling, the cook clutched instinctively at an enamel table which upset with a metallic clatter. There were exclamations of alarm from the living room.

"This is it!" said Gulliver, picking up a chair in one hand, while with the other he grabbed the handle of a teakettle that had been simmering on the stove. As he came out of the kitchen and turned toward the living room, Whiz Walton and the others were right behind him.

Miguel appeared at the archway holding his long-bladed knife. He screamed in surprise when he saw that the prisoners were free. His arm moved like a striking serpent and the knife spun through the air.

Gulliver brought up the chair like a shield, just in time. The knife struck the bottom of the seat and stayed there. After the long enforced silence, Gulliver welcomed the opportunity to use his voice. He made the most of it.

"Yo' slimy breed!" he bellowed. "Yo' been needin' a bath for a long time, an' here she is!"

The kettle full of boiling water flew in Miguel's direction and crashed against the wall next to the half-breed's head. The lid flew off and Miguel screamed in agony as the scalding water doused his face and shoulders.

Gulliver was on the move, charging forward with the chair held so that the legs stuck out in front.

Miguel was rammed to one side as Gulliver burst into the living room followed by Lou Gates, Whiz Walton, Tom Quest, and his father.

CHAPTER 28

Fight to the Finish

GULLIVER'S RUSH had sent Miguel against the wall. Lou Gates, right behind Gulliver, clipped the half-breed on the chin with his fist. In the living room the card players leaped to their feet and went for their guns, but had to scramble to dodge the chair that Gulliver threw into their midst.

Four guns barked almost simultaneously. Two of the gunmen fired, but their shots were hurried and went wild. Whiz Walton and Lou Gates squeezed the triggers of their pistols at the same time, aiming low. One of the bullets caught a gunman in the leg. He fell with a yell of pain as Gulliver closed in on the others. The next instant found the big man, Lou Gates, and Whiz Walton in a melee with the swarthy-skinned thugs.

Tom Quest saw Huddlebeck reaching for a weapon in a gun case on the wall.

"No you don't!" he cried, running forward.

Huddlebeck turned from the case with a pistol in one hand. He fired—just as Tom Quest left the ground in a flying tackle learned on the football field. He could almost hear the bullet zip past his head just before his shoulder slammed into Huddlebeck's knees.

Huddlebeck went down with a cry of rage. In throwing out his hands to break his fall, the gun flew from his fingers and skidded across the floor to a corner where Morton crouched in abject fear. Morton saw the gun and picked it up. Holding it in both hands, he aimed in the general direction of the archway and squeezed the trigger. The bullet caught Hamilton Quest in one shoulder with force enough to turn him half around before he fell. Another gun cracked in the midst of the struggle in the center of the room.

"Try to shoot me, will yo'!" bellowed Gulliver. He brought his fist down like a pile driver squarely on the top of one man's head.

Whiz Walton was half-stunned, and Lou Gates lay unconscious with blood seeping from a gash above one ear. Gulliver was left to battle the remaining gunman who was able-bodied, in addition to the one who had a bullet in the leg.

Meanwhile, Tom found himself overmatched with

Hector Huddlebeck. Huddlebeck was big and strong, and had kept himself in excellent condition. He had a grip on Tom Quest's throat, and Tom's arms were working like pistons, driving blow after blow against Huddlebeck's hard stomach, but each blow was weaker. Tom felt lightheaded and knew that he could not continue long with the choking fingers on his throat.

No one knew it at the time, but the bullet that had so narrowly missed Gulliver had drilled through Morton's forehead. Morton lay face down on the floor, a gun still clutched in both dead hands.

Tom tried to cling to the last shimmering trace of consciousness. With one desperate spurt of strength he managed to raise his arms and slam both sides of Huddlebeck's head simultaneously with the heels of his cupped hands. He put all the force he had left into the twin blows, and he didn't feel the choking fingers suddenly relax. Tom was already unconscious.

When Tom Quest opened his eyes, he saw the battered face of Gulliver and heard his big friend's voice.

"Yo', Tom," said Gulliver anxiously. "Yo' all right?"

Tom felt weak, and his throat was sore and stiff, but he said, "I—I guess so." He sat up and looked around the room. "It—it's all over!"

"Yo' been unconscious for over half an hour, Tom."

"There—there was lots of gunplay. What—what happened?"

"Now, take it easy, Tom, an' I'll give yo' the facts in short order. Yo' dad had his shoulder brushed by a bullet, but it's not serious."

"Dad! Where is he!"

"Right here, son."

Tom turned and saw his father on his other side.

"Lou Gates an' Whiz Walton," Gulliver continued, "got beat up some, but nothin' serious. A critter named Morton is dead, an' one o' the gunslingers has a bullet in the leg. The rest, includin' Huddlebeck an' the cook in the kitchen, was just beat up so we could hogtie them. The feller who went after the dogs come back lookin' disgusted and found a nice surprise party waitin' for him."

Tom looked about the big room. Morton lay beneath a blanket in the corner, but there was no one else in sight.

"Where is everyone?"

"We lugged 'em into bedrooms an' wired their hands an' feet to bunks so's they'd keep out o' trouble."

Whiz Walton and Lou Gates came into the big living room.

"How's Tom?" asked the columnist.

"I'm all right," replied the boy, getting to his feet.

"I have news for you," said Whiz. "Huddlebeck has squealed."

"About what?"

The reporter drew a small sheet of paper from his hip

pocket and unfolded it. "This is a statement," Whiz explained. "Huddlebeck names Miguel as the one who
killed Wahkee."

"Everyone in this house," said Hamilton Quest, "had
a share in that. They are all murderers, including Huddlebeck himself! As soon as they had captured Tom, they
intended to set fire to this place. All of us would have
been killed and Huddlebeck would have claimed that it
was an accident. That fiend was ready to commit five
more murders to cover the murder of Wahkee!"

"Well, anyway," the columnist said, "he names
Miguel as the one who finally killed Wahkee. Also as
the one who put the dynamite in the truck to kill Gleason. Here's his signed statement. Lou Gates and I signed
as witnesses."

Hamilton Quest read the document carefully. "How,"
he said, returning it to Whiz Walton, "did you get him
to make this statement?"

"Very simple. We told him we were taking him back
to the Indian village, and that if he would sign a statement, we'd turn him over to the law, but if he didn't,
we'd let the Indians take over. He knew what to expect
from *them* in retaliation for the murder of Wahkee."

"What are we going to do about the prisoners?" Tom
Quest asked. "Take them all back to the Indian village,
or leave them tied up here?"

Whiz suggested that a litter be improvised, on which

the body of Wahkee could be carried. "We'll take Huddlebeck and the cook along to carry the litter. They're in better condition than the others. Mr. Quest probably can persuade War-rah-pa to send men here to collect the others while one of us drives to the nearest telephone and calls the sheriff's office."

The suggestion was briefly discussed, and then adopted. A folding cot made of canvas and light wood was found in a closet. It would serve admirably as a stretcher. Wahkee's body, wrapped in a blanket, was placed on the litter. Then Huddlebeck and the cook were untied and told what they were to do.

"Now, I guess," said Whiz Walton, "we're all set to go back to the village."

Hamilton Quest sighed deeply. "This," he said, "is the end of an expedition that has failed."

"Failed?" repeated Tom Quest. "What do you mean, Dad? Huddlebeck won't bother the Mandans any more."

"No matter what happens to Huddlebeck, son, someone else—perhaps other members of the syndicate—will take over the uranium-bearing land. After all, Huddlebeck's organization has a title to the land which will stand up in court unless the Mandan Stone is found."

"Doggone," grumbled Gulliver, "that's so. We ain't got no idea where the stone is at. Wahkee was the only one who knew, an' he's dead. Why, doggone it," he continued, turning toward Hamilton Quest, "without we find that stone, we can't clear yo' name!"

"Not only that," said Tom. "Whiz Walton is out of a job."

"Don't worry about me," said the columnist.

"But at least we are all alive," Hamilton Quest pointed out. "That is more than I dared hope for a few hours ago."

Gulliver had found and strapped on his own gun belt. He directed Huddlebeck and the cook to pick up the litter and start toward the Mandan village. Whiz Walton went ahead carrying a flashlight. Lou Gates walked at Gulliver's side while Tom Quest and his father followed.

CHAPTER 29

The Hidden Stone

It was daylight when the party came out of the woods and reached the place where the cars had been left.

"To save time," suggested Lou Gates, "how would it be if I took Mr. Quest's car and drove to the nearest telephone? I can call the sheriff's office, and then we'll get rid of the prisoners."

"Good idea!" said Whiz Walton. "The sooner the better. I'm just about worn out."

"We all are," Hamilton Quest said. "Remember, we have been two nights without sleep."

"It's all right then to take your car, Mr. Quest?"

"Of course it is, Gates. Go ahead. The rest of us will go to War-rah-pa's lodge."

Strangely enough, War-rah-pa was not surprised to learn that his son was dead. He stood in the doorway of the lodge. The aged chief had learned by some psychic

206

power what to expect, and he had put on full ceremonial regalia to receive the body in accordance with Mandan tradition. Mah-to stood at his side. And lining the perimeter of the council circle stood hundreds of still, impassive Indians, their faces immobile but their keen dark eyes following the litter as the body of their young chief was carried to his father's lodge.

War-rah-pa wore an elaborate headdress of eagle feathers similar to other Indian war bonnets. The tail dangled to the ground. The headgear was topped by the curving horns of a buffalo—symbolic of a chief. In his hand War-rah-pa held a spear about seven feet in length. At intervals from the stone tip to the far end of the spear, eagle feathers had been tied.

When the cot was placed on the ground in front of the doorway of the lodge, War-rah-pa pointed to the blanketed form and said, "Wahkee."

Hamilton Quest replied. "He gave his life, War-rah-pa, rather than break his promise to me."

"Who kill?" demanded the chief, looking sternly at Hector Huddlebeck.

"The ones who killed will be punished by the white man's law."

"You promise?"

What Hamilton Quest said to him in the Mandan tongue satisfied War-rah-pa.

Meanwhile, Whiz Walton and Gulliver tied the hands

of Huddlebeck and the cook with lengths of cord they had brought for that purpose.

"We'll leave 'em right here on the ground," said Gulliver, " 'til the lawmen come. I'll get Fatty, so's they'll all be here together."

The fat man was just waking from the effects of the sleeping potion when Gulliver crossed the flagstone floor of the lodge.

"Now what?" he growled in a thick and sleepy voice.

"What's it to yo'?" retorted Gulliver, gripping the prisoner by the belt.

The sun was just beginning to appear when Gulliver dropped the fat man unceremoniously beside Huddlebeck and the cook.

"I hope," he said, looking at the flabby torso, "yo' got to wait all day for the law. An' I hope that sun is downright scorchin'. The pasty hide o' yo' will git downright sunburned. I—"

Gulliver broke off at a sharp exclamation from Tom Quest. The boy rushed forward, gripped the fat man's elbow, and swung him to the side.

"What's the matter with yo', Tom?" demanded Gulliver.

"I saw something!" Tom pointed to the soft flesh of the upper arm just below the shoulder. "Look!" he exclaimed.

An impression about an inch in height was clearly visible. It was a spiral shape, similar to the Archimedian pattern on the rings that Tom and Gulliver wore. It was pressed in the flesh much as the indentations of a rumpled pillow sometimes appear on the cheek of one who has slept without moving.

"How do you account for that?" asked Whiz Walton.

Hamilton Quest was examining the spiral. "That looks," he said, "like the pattern I scratched on the reverse side of the Mandan Stone."

"Wait!" cried Tom. "I have an idea!" He rushed into the lodge and crossed the flagstones to the place where the fat man had been sleeping.

Whiz Walton and Gulliver raced after him. Hamilton Quest followed more slowly, and War-rah-pa watched from the doorway.

Tom's voice trembled with excitement. "Wahkee hid the stone in plain sight!" he said. "Look here!" He pointed to a big slab among the other flagstones in the floor. In one corner the spiral had been scratched with a sharp instrument.

"Don't you get it?" Tom said. "Wahkee took up a flagstone and put this in its place. He crated the stone he removed. That's the one he gave to Gates and Gleason. That's the one that was stolen from the truck and later replaced with the second counterfeit."

Gulliver snatched the nearest spear from the wall and forced the point under one end of the stone.

"We'll darn soon find out!" he said. "When I pry 'er up, yo' flip 'er over." He pressed down on the long handle of the spear. Tom Quest and Whiz clawed at the edge of the stone as it was raised, then lifted it to its end.

"Careful!" said Hamilton Quest. "Don't let it drop!"

"Let 'er down easy!" Gulliver ordered.

The stone was lowered face up—and there, for all to see, were words in a strange language which, when translated, defined the boundaries of the land that had been given by the government to the Mandan Indians.

It took but a moment for Hamilton Quest to scrutinize the face of the stone and confirm the fact that it was the one he had pronounced authentic. There were tears in his eyes as he rose. "This," he said, "will restore my reputation, but Wahkee paid too dearly."

"Holy mackerel!" Whiz Walton exclaimed. "This is the story of the year! I'm back in business again!"

It was a week before the party left the Mandan village. The sheriff and his men had come and taken charge of the prisoners. The two Great Danes had been brought to the village and in almost no time at all had adopted Tom Quest. Whether he liked it or not, Tom was their master. Whiz Walton had telephoned his paper and received enthusiastic congratulations from the publisher himself.

Hamilton Quest had called the University and told them he was bringing back the real Mandan Stone.

The future looked bright for everyone, including Lou Gates, who was going to take charge of the mining project as soon as the legal claim of the Indians to the property had been established.

The Mandan Stone was on the floor of Gulliver's jeep, carefully wrapped in blankets. Tom Quest was driving, with Gulliver at his side and Whiz Walton in back.

Hamilton Quest and Lou Gates were in the other car, a few yards ahead of the jeep. Two wet noses pressed close to the rear window, as two Great Danes watched to make sure that Tom Quest remained in view.

Gulliver chuckled. "Looks like we got us a couple o' dogs," he said to Tom. "Or vice versa."

Visiting Gulliver's Texas ranch, Tom Quest finds an abandoned gold mine, rumored to be haunted. What he discovers—and the terrific outcome of that discovery—is a story you won't want to miss!

THE SECRET OF THUNDER MOUNTAIN